SABRES OF THE REICH

The Black Cossacks Series
Book Two

Charles Whiting
writing as
Leo Kessler

SAPERE
BOOKS

SABRES OF THE REICH

Published by Sapere Books.

24 Trafalgar Road, Ilkley, LS29 8HH

saperebooks.com

ISBN: 978-0-85495-511-4

'The human heart is the starting point of all matters
pertaining to war.'

Marechal de Saxe, 1732.

THE COSSACKS ARE COMING!

The terrified cry sprang from mouth to mouth. In an instant the panic-stricken peasants scattered, running for the village, dropping their rakes and hay forks as they did so. A few wild shots and the soldiers in their earth coloured blouses had dropped their rifles and were pelting after them in wild flight.

The horde of howling, fur-hatted men, crouched low over the flying manes of their sweat lathered horses, hit the village at full gallop. Hooves thundered over the cobbles. Sabres, already dripping bright red with blood, flashed time and time again. Screaming with agony, peasants and Red Army men disappeared under flying hooves. With the Cossacks' sabres whistling about their ears, and the hot breath of the gasping horses on their necks, the survivors dived for cover, crouching terrified, as the laughing, triumphant horsemen started to loot their village.

Minutes later yet another Red Army strongpoint had been destroyed and the half-wild horsemen, their shaggy little ponies laden down with loot, were riding hell-for-leather for the infinite Russian fir forest from which they had emerged so frighteningly...

It had always been thus. Ever since their 'Little Father', the Czar, had made the half-wild frontier people his own special élite cavalry, with every single male Cossack recruited into the Imperial Army at the age of 18, to serve for twenty long years in one of the five Cossack hordes: the Don, the Kuban, the Ural, the Orenburg and the Terek. Although their Little Father admired his Cossacks for their horsemanship, their bravery, and their martial skill, his workers and peasants feared them. Violence was part of the warrior nation's way of life and they could always be relied upon by the Czar to put down a strike, a riot, a revolution with their gleaming sabres and cruel many-lashed knouts.

In 1918 when the workers and peasants came to power and their Little Father was dead, murdered in the cellars of his own summer palace, they paid back their debt of blood. The Cossacks were slaughtered in their thousands. Their lands were seized from them, and they were driven into the mountains to eke out a desperate existence as outlaws, with every man's hand against them; or forced into exile to become the new Jews, wandering over the face of Europe, finding a home nowhere, dreaming with nostalgia and longing of their lost homelands.

All that had changed in 1942. Reichsführer SS, Heinrich Himmler, the most feared man in German-occupied Europe, desperate to fill the great gaps in the German frontline in Russia, had recalled the one-time warrior people. The survivors, eager to pay off the old score, rallied to the crooked cross banner in their thousands. Outlaws, émigrés, deserters from the Red Army, ex-prisoners of war, all of them joined to fight against their Russian brothers in the ranks of the oppressors.

Clothed in the drab field-grey of the Wehrmacht, they still draped themselves in the trappings of Imperial Russia: the Persian lamb fur hat, knee-length boots, the flowing capes, the great curved moustaches, the jewel encrusted daggers and sabres which had been handed down for generations.

And how they had fought! None more so than the Commander of the Black Cossacks from the Don, General Alexei Bogdan. Wherever his marauding horsemen appeared and the cry went up 'the Cossacks are coming!', their enemies in the Red Army fled in absolute panic. The name of Black Cossack alone sufficed. For two whole years between 1942 and 1944, Bogdan's feared, half-wild riders had held back the Red Army advance; time and time again they had saved the situation with their dash, their bravery, their blood.

But now the summer of 1944 had arrived. After three years of cruel occupation, the Russians had finally driven the German invaders from their war-torn soil. Now the Red Army had advanced well into Poland. In their millions, the victorious Russians streamed westwards, smashing everything in front of them, beating back the Germans relentlessly, pushing them kilometre by kilometre ever closer to their own German homeland.

Now all that stood in their way was the broad, fast running River Vistula, the great Polish capital city of Warsaw — and General Alexei Bogdan's Division of Black Cossacks...

Leo Kessler.

BOOK ONE: *REVOLT ON THE VISTULA*

'I am sure you all know the terrible risk we are taking in beginning this rising... But it is now or never.'

General Bor to his Staff, August 1st, 1944.

CHAPTER 1

'Black Cossacks — *halt*!'

'Halt, little brothers ... halt!' Hurriedly the whispered command passed from mouth to mouth. Now they were nearly out of the thick Polish fir forest, which bordered the River Vistula. Before them lay the baking plain and the whole might of the Red Army. Urgently the men of the Black Cossack Division, filtering through the firs everywhere, reigned in their tired, sweating mounts and waited for what must come soon. There was no sound save the harsh breathing of the horses and the faint cries of the drunken Russian cavalrymen camped in the plain beyond.

So far General Bogdan's plan had worked perfectly. At dusk they had left the Fritz positions around Warsaw, had ridden hard southwards, crossing the broad Vistula under the cover of darkness and had spent most of this day working their way through the forest, so that they were now in position at the joint between the First and Second White Russian Fronts. Their lean, handsome commander General Alexei Bogdan had explained their bold mission behind the Red Army's lines, thus: 'Although the two armies are fighting shoulder to shoulder, at the joint between them their command structures are at least fifty kilometres apart. We'll hit them there — hard and fast. By the time their neighbouring division is given the alarm by its Army HQ, we'll have been long back across the Vistula and the 5th Red Cossack Division' — he had grinned suddenly at the assembled soldiers, fur cap tilted rakishly on the side of his gleaming black curls, long Russian cigarette jutting from the corner of his mouth — '*will be listening to the bats playing saxophones*!'

But now General Bogdan, riding at the head of his Black Cossacks, like a simple soldier on scout duty and not the divisional commander, was no longer grinning. His harsh, masterful face, marred only by a trace of bitterness around the mouth, was set and determined. 'Let's go and have a look at the drunken Red bastards, Peter,' he grunted to the Division's one-armed German liaison officer. Baron Peter von Kranz had once rescued him from Kazan Concentration Camp.

Easily the two officers swung themselves off their lathered horses, and creeping to the edge of the forest, focused their binoculars on the plain below.

Already it was beginning to grow dark. Behind them the blood-red ball of the summer sun was slipping into the Vistula and the dark shadows of the night were starting to slide across the parched plain. But the two observers, hidden in the resin-scented trees, could make out the enemy positions well enough. Mostly the Red Cossacks were sprawled out in the yellow grass in front of their pup tents, drinking the last of their weekly vodka ration. But some of them were still active, jumping their sweating, panting horses over high barred fences, while two half-naked Cossacks lashed out in drunken anger with a great iron bar at any horse which threatened to jump too low.

'Typical bad Cossack tricks, little brother,' Bogdan growled angrily to the broadfaced, blond German officer. 'I know them all — a piece of barbed wire under the saddle, or fixed inside the bit, or a knout filled with nails to make the poor animal run faster.' He spat contemptuously into the leaves. 'Trash like that don't deserve the name Cossack!'

Peter von Kranz lowered his glasses and nodded agreement. 'What now, General?'

Bogdan forgot the Red Cossacks' drunken cruelty at once. He rose to his feet and tugged at his flamboyant, black, wide-skirted *Cherkesska*. 'We wait until it is dark, Peter, and then,' the Cossack General's dark eyes gleamed, 'we slaughter them where they lay.'

In spite of the heat of the summer day, Peter von Kranz shuddered.

A low summer mist covered the plain now. Like grey wolves, the Black Cossacks crept closer and closer to their prey. Every few minutes the leading horsemen, their horses' hooves muffled in rags, would halt, the mist swirling up about their legs as they strained their ears. But there was no sound to indicate that the drunken Red Cossacks were aware of their presence.

Bogdan, positioned in the centre of the long line of cavalry, touched the little leather sack he wore around his neck. Peter recognised the sign. The sack contained earth from his native Don. Wherever the big General might be killed, the earth would be thrown in his grave so that, according to the Cossack custom, he would be buried in his 'native soil'. Bogdan always touched it to reassure himself that it was still there just before he went into action. It wouldn't be long now.

Another five minutes passed. The lead scouts stumbled into a machine gun post, filled with drunken, snoring Red Army men. Their throats were slit before they were aware what was happening to them. The Black Cossacks moved on towards the sleeping camp.

A flare hissed into the grey sky. It hung there for what seemed an age bathing the Black Cossacks, who had frozen into immobility, in its blood-red light. Peter von Kranz at Bogdan's side hardly breathed, his body tense and expectant, waiting for the first angry snarl of a Red Army machine gun. But none came. Finally the flare sank to the ground and died in the mist. The Cossacks crept closer and closer to the little tents. They passed through a copse of trees, the twigs cracking like pistol shots under their horses' hooves, the low hanging branches clawing at their set faces. Just behind Bogdan a young Cossack, taken by surprise, dropped his sabre with a clatter.

'Son of a whore!' Bogdan hissed angrily, swinging round on the unfortunate boy. 'I'll have the eggs off you with your own sabre if you do that again!'

They passed another couple of murdered Red Army men: one with a Cossack knife thrust between his shoulders; the other, his face a contorted crimson, his tongue hanging out like a piece of leather, the thin wire with which the scout had strangled him biting deeply into his neck. Bogdan nodded his approval. His Cossack scouts had not forgotten the cruel, cunning traditions of their half-wild forefathers, who had been the Czar's most feared troops.

Now the tops of the little Red Army tents loomed up above the grey mist, only a matter of metres away. Carefully Bogdan drew his sabre and wrapped the leather strap around his wrist, scarred with the sword slashes of a quarter of a century of cavalry combat. He took a deep breath and raised himself high in his stirrups.

'*STOP*!' A sentry challenged suddenly.

They had been spotted after all!

Bogdan did not hesitate. 'Black Cossacks,' he yelled urgently, as the first burst of red tracer cut the air angrily, '*charge*!'

He dug his stirrups into the sides of his mount. The great white stallion responded at once. Its ears pressed flat against its head, its neck quivering, the long silken mane flying behind it, it leapt forward. Bogdan was seized by the old elation, which banished all fear, reason, logic; overcome by the old atavistic Cossack desire to kill. Screaming crazy obscenities his Black Cossacks, crouched low over their horses' necks, sabres pointing straight ahead, charged with him, full out.

It was a massacre. The Cossacks hit the tents at full gallop, sending them to the ground, slashing and chopping at the drunken, helpless occupants without mercy as they fought to free themselves from the canvas.

An officer with the great stiff epaulettes of a staff colonel tried to bar Peter's progress. The one-armed German, the reins of his mount gripped between his teeth, fired instinctively. The Red Army officer's face shattered into fragments like broken glass, but he didn't go down until Boris, the Black Cossacks' Chief of Staff, with an exultant shriek sliced off his shattered head with one great sweep of his sabre. The Red fell to the ground, blood gushing from his neck, like water from a burst pipe.

A half-naked giant grabbed at Bogdan's foot and tried to drag him from his mount. The cursing swaying mêlée all around was too tight for Bogdan to use his sabre. He jabbed his spur directly into the giant's face, who fell back screaming, his right eye gouged out. Bogdan had no mercy. Savagely he tugged at the bit. The stallion whinnied frantically and reared up, its forelegs flailing the air in pain. Bogdan loosened the bit. An instant later one ton of man and mount crashed down upon the blinded soldier. His dead body was pressed into the bath of blood in which the crazed Cossacks wallowed like animals, slashing, gouging, hacking; overcome by a frenzy of killing.

'They're getting away, General,' Boris yelled urgently.

Bogdan swung his horse round. A group of Red Cossacks had hurled themselves onto their unsaddled mounts and were making a break for it, bowling over their own men in a wild, panicky desire to escape.

'After me!' Bogdan commanded and thrust his spurs into his stallion's flanks. The success of his plan depended upon no one being allowed to escape and alarm Army HQ before the Black Cossack Division were safely back on the other side of the Vistula.

Peter von Kranz jerked the trigger of his pistol. Scarlet flame stabbed the darkness. A Red Cossack screamed hysterically. The slug flung him out of the saddle, his terrified horse careering on without him.

Crouched low over his horse's head, Bogdan, his face wild with excitement, came level with the rear enemy soldier. The man swung round and tried to shoot him. Bogdan did not give him a chance to fire. His sabre hissed through the air and the man's hand fell to the ground, still clutching the unfired pistol. Bogdan swung the blood-red sword through the air once again, and brought it down across the man's far shoulder. He screamed with agony as the blade bit deep into his muscles. A second later, loosing his grip on the horse's mane, he flew to the ground to be trampled to death under the hooves of the Cossacks' horses.

Riding parallel with Bogdan was Boris, a terrifying sight, with his hideously scarred lobster-pink mask of a face, the result of a tank accident in 1941. He gripped his reins between his stainless steel teeth and raised the Schmeisser machine pistol hanging around his neck. With no time to take careful aim, he fired a wild burst into the backs of the fleeing Red Army men. At that range the volley of 9mm slugs swept them from their horses like a gigantic punch. Not one escaped.

Bogdan reigned his horse, his chest heaving madly, his eyes gleaming with wild, almost sexual excitement. 'Enough, enough!' he commanded, raising his blood dripping sabre high into the air. 'Let the horses go.' He nodded to the men lying on the ground. 'Finish off the bastards who aren't yet dead!'

At the walk, he turned, and followed by his staff began to make his way back to the surprised camp.

The wrecked camp was silent now, save for the groans of the wounded and the regular dry crack of the revolvers, as slaughter squads moved from prisoner to prisoner blowing them neatly to eternity. A few of the Black Cossacks were already beginning to loot the bodies, some of them armed with the great pincers, used by the Division's blacksmiths, to extract the senior officer's gold teeth. Peter von Kranz shivered, but General Bogdan watched the looters' activities dispassionately. It had been the Cossacks' privilege to loot the dead after battle for centuries, ever since the Czar had bribed the Cossack hordes to become his pathfinders and irregular cavalry, in the new unexplored territories in the east and south.

Boris cantered up and saluted.

'Yes?' Bogdan transferred his gaze from a burly Cossack who had lodged his muddy boot under the chin of a dead Red officer and grunting with effort was trying to extract a gold tooth from his upper set.

'Casualties, General.'

Bogdan frowned. 'Many?'

'Twenty killed and fifty wounded, General.'

16

Bogdan beamed at Peter von Kranz. 'Did you hear that, little brother?' he asked enthusiastically. 'We've wiped out a whole Red division — five thousand men — for the price of a handful of ours. By the Holy Virgin of Kazan, I don't think even that constipated, long-faced Himmler of yours will have anything to complain about this time, eh?'

The one-armed Baron grinned at the Cossack's description of the most feared man in Europe, Reichsführer SS Heinrich Himmler. 'No, I don't think he will, sir.' Then he was businesslike again. He pointed at the sudden flurry of signal flares shooting up into the night sky on the horizon. 'But I don't think we've much time left to sit on our laurels and congratulate ourselves, if I may say so.'

'You may, little brother,' Bogdan said easily, pleased with himself and his victory. He stared for a moment at the newly agitated sky and nodded his agreement. 'Yes, you are right. Those fat base stallions over there are worried about what's going on up here. They want to know why the 5th Red Cavalry Division is not replying to their radio signals.' He smiled. 'We could tell them, couldn't we, Peter? But I think we'd better leave them to find out for themselves… One thing is certain,' he rubbed a big dirty hand across his face, 'this night's work will set Comrade Marshal Rokossovsky's plans for crossing the Vistula back a few days. You Fritzes will be able to hold on to your precious Warsaw for a little while longer, and we shall be able to enjoy the undeniable pleasure of fumbling beneath a few more Polish petticoats before the Reds attack.' He raised his voice and barked at Boris. 'Major, give the order for the Division to move back across the Vistula — at once!'

'Sir!' The Chief of Staff raised his bloody sabre to his lips in salute, and swung his horse around.

Minutes later, the jubilant Black Cossacks, laden down with their booty, disappeared back into the grey summer mist as swiftly as they had appeared, leaving behind them the slowly stiffening bodies of their cruelly massacred brothers.

CHAPTER 2

On that hot afternoon of August 1st, 1944, while General Bogdan was leading his weary Black Cossacks back to their quarters south of Warsaw, another General was making his way up the capital's Pawia Street. But this General was not dressed in a bemedalled, colourful uniform. He wore a shabby raincoat and a civilian hat. The only weapon he possessed was a small pistol hidden deep in his back pocket, and as he passed the German sentry outside a pillbox guarding the exit to the street, he lowered his gaze humbly, as befitted a member of a conquered people. Nevertheless, this shabby Polish General, with the skinny figure and balding head, was going to war again after five long years of hardship, frustration and repression.

Carefully the General knocked three times on the wooden door of the butter-coloured building, which before the war had been a tobacco factory. The door was opened almost immediately by a hard-eyed giant, his hand clutching a pistol behind his back. 'Bor,' snapped the shabby General, 'I am expected.'

The giant sprang to attention. 'General!' he rapped. Lieutenant Kamler, in charge of the factory HQ, pistol clearly visible in his belt, pushed the giant aside. 'This way, sir,' he said quickly. 'They're all waiting for you upstairs.' His eyes gleamed with youthful excitement. 'It won't be long now, sir, will it?'

General Tadeusz Komorowski, alias Bor, commander of the Polish Secret Army, looked at the young officer almost sadly, wondering if the man knew what he was really letting himself in for on this hot August afternoon. Then he dismissed the thought. 'What is the situation next door, Lieutenant?' he asked business like again, indicating the German strongpoint across the way, visible through the dirty window.

'The Fritzes have raised the garrison to fifty men and they've got a couple of machine guns in position. But I've got men out in the yard, armed withgrenades, watching their every move.'

'I see,' Bor answered thoughtfully. He knew he was taking a calculated risk, situating his battle HQ next to a German strongpoint, but he banked on the Gestapo never suspecting that the nerve centre of the uprising would be located within fifty metres of one of their own positions. By the time they found out, it would be too late. 'But remember, Kamler, not one move before five.' He raised his finger in warning. 'Then you can attack them.'

Kamler grinned boyishly. 'We've waited five years for this, sir. I reckon we can wait another fifty minutes.'

Bor grinned faintly, too, and climbed the stairs. Eagerly his staff officers and the radio operators crowding the upper room, sprang to attention when he entered. But he waved for them to be seated and asked without ceremony, 'Well?'

Brigadier Tadeusz Pelczynski, his Chief of Staff, replied, stabbing his finger at the big map of Warsaw on the table in front of him to emphasise his points. 'All units of the AK are reported in position, sir. At the Vistula bridges, the airport, the radio station, police and army HQs.'

'Stahel's HQ?' Bor asked, referring to Marshal Rainer Stahel, the new military governor of Warsaw.

Brigadier Pelczynski nodded. 'We have two companies of storm troops ready to go at zero hour, sir.'

'Good.' Bor flashed a glance at his wristwatch, all that he had left of his personal jewellery; the rest had long gone on the black market in these last five terrible years of German occupation. There were still forty minutes to go. 'Gentlemen,' he said carefully. 'I am sure you all know the terrible risk we are taking in beginning this rising. We are outnumbered by the Fritzes five to one, and we must consider the fate of the city's million civilians if indiscriminate firing breaks out in the capital.' He sighed, fully conscious of his terrible responsibility, after all these months of planning. 'But it is a risk we must take. It is now or never. The Russians are on the other side of the Vistula, and the Fritzes won't be able to hold them for ever. Once again we Poles will be faced by a Russian invasion. But this time, gentlemen' — suddenly there was iron in his voice — 'our capital will be in Polish hands when the Russians march in. That way we shall have some say in our own future until our comrades in London return and lend us their support.'

There was a murmur of agreement from the assembled staff officers.

'Sir,' Brigadier Pelczynski said, 'I feel confident we'll pull it off even with the unskilled troops at our disposal. At five o'clock when the factories end the day shift and the night shift begins to go on, no-one will suspect the presence of so many young people on the streets, in the proximity of the Fritz strongpoints throughout the city. After all, we've worked on this plan for months. I believe we'll catch the Fritzes with their trousers down this time,' he allowed himself a smile, 'and we'll give them a nice hefty kick up their fat German arses!'

Bor returned his smile. 'Brigadier, I hope that —' He broke off suddenly. Outside a rifle had cracked. Someone screamed shrilly.

'Look out, sir!' a radioman near the window yelled urgently. The window shattered. Slugs careened off the walls suddenly, showering the surprised staff officers with brick and plaster.

Bor rushed to the shattered window. Down below a German truck blocked the entrance to the factory HQ, its dead driver slumped across his steering wheel behind a spider's web of broken glass. Everywhere Kamler's men were running to take up their positions, German machine gun bullets stitching a deadly blue pattern on the cobbles all around their feet, as another enemy truck, filled with German security police rumbled towards the factory gate. Its intention was obvious; it was going to barrel its way in.

Bor's heart sank. If the Fritzes broke through, his HQ might well be captured before the uprising had even got underway. But he reckoned without Kamler's men. Braving the enemy machine gun fire, which was lashing the whole length of the factory wall, an AK man smashed open a window and lobbed a grenade into the back of the open truck.

A moment later the AK man fell back, his stomach ripped wide open, dying. But he had done his job well. With a thick muffled crump, the grenade exploded. Security policemen were tossed high in the air, arms and legs flailing, like crazy puppets. The driver, his backbone shattered by the force of the explosion, lost control of the truck. It careened off the road. With a crash that made the factory floor tremble under Bor's feet, the truck struck the nearest wall. An instant later, it burst into flames, swamping the dead and dying policemen in the back with a wave of burning petrol.

A great cheer rang up from Kamler's excited young men. They had achieved their first victory.

'Sir!'

Bor swung round. It was Pelczynski, his hair covered in white plaster. 'What is it?'

The Chief of Staff grinned stupidly. 'Can't you hear, sir?' Bor cocked his head to one side. Suddenly he heard it: the rising tide of explosions, orchestrated by the savage hiss of automatic fire. He recognised the sound immediately. Everywhere his young men and women, some not much more than children, had begun their action, rushing the German strongpoints, ambushing their trucks, blocking the main roads. 'Quick, let's go on the roof, Pelczynski!' he yelled above the ever increasing sound of battle.

Hurriedly the two generals ran up the narrow stairs to the roof. Outside the German machine guns, only fifteen metres away, were still pouring a vicious hail of fire into the factory. But the two generals had no time to be afraid, nor had Kamler's men stationed there. All their eyes were fixed on the flag flying over the tallest building in Warsaw, the 16-storey Prudential Building, which dominated the city centre.

'Our flag, sir,' Pelczynski breathed, devouring the red and white eagle of Poland which now flew proudly over the city centre. 'And they're everywhere, sir. The town hall … savings bank tower … the library…'

Bor swallowed hard. This was a great moment for him. The skinny, balding ex-cavalry officer, with the melancholy expression and small clipped moustache, had waited five years for it ever since he'd been persuaded not to go into exile, after the September defeat but to remain behind in Poland and form the Secret Army. Now the moment had arrived. The Polish Eagle flew over the Polish capital again, for the first time since 1939!

Bor fought back his tears. There was no time for emotion now. As the flag flying so proudly over the Prudential Building started to disappear into the rising smoke of battle, and the roar of the new war grew louder by the minute, he clattered down the narrow stairs into his operations room.

Everywhere the radio operators tensed over their radios, waiting to spread the word to every city throughout German occupied Poland. And to the world.

But first Bor had a message for his own soldiers. Swiftly the sweating operators began to rap it out on the morse keys. 'Soldiers of the capital! I have today issued the order which you desire, for open warfare against Poland's age-old enemy, the German invader. After nearly five years of ceaseless and determined struggle, carried on in secret, you stand openly with arms in hand, to restore freedom in our country and to mete out fitting punishment to the German criminals, for the terror and crime committed by them on Polish soil...'

The Warsaw Uprising had begun!

CHAPTER 3

'*What did you say?*' Reichsführer Heinrich Himmler bellowed across the desk.

The black-clad giant aide paled. 'Reichsführer, we have just heard from 9th Army HQ at Cracow that the Poles have revolted in Warsaw.' He gulped and stepped back a pace, almost as if he expected the bespectacled, moon-faced head of the SS would strike him there and then.

Beside himself with sudden rage, Himmler flung down his pen. 'You mean that those miserable sewer-rats, that Slavic scum, the Polack pack, has had the audacity to raise their dirty paws against the Greater German Wehrmacht!'

'Yessir,' the SS aide answered miserably. 'According to 9th Army HQ, they are attacking all our strongpoints in the old city — mostly successfully.'

'*Das ist doch zum Kotzen!*' Himmler cried thickly and rose to his feet. Forgetting the aide's presence, he paced the room in his too-big boots, tugging at his collar, taking off and replacing his pince-nez, running a limp hand across his sallow, sweat-glazed face, and muttering to himself. Abruptly he halted in mid-stride and rapped a question at the aide. 'What kind of troops have we in the capital — SS?'

'No, Reichsführer — mostly police formations and several Wehrmacht battalions — infantry. Though I believe Marshal Stahel has an SS formation guarding his own HQ. But for the most part —'

Himmler motioned him to be quiet. 'This is a job for the SS,' he cried impatiently. 'Those weak sisters of the Regular Army don't know how to tackle such a task. Those Polacks are animals which have had the damned audacity to show their teeth to their masters. Only my SS know how to ram their rotten yellow teeth down their stinking throats.' His mind suddenly made up he cried, 'Heinz, get my cap and belt — I'm going to see the Führer about this. He'll give me the order I need to wipe that Polack rabble from the face of the earth for good.'

Hitler was still deathly pale from the attempt on his life eleven days before, and his left arm, burnt when the bomb had exploded in his East Prussian HQ, was bound up in a sling. Almost apathetically, he listened to Himmler's angry account of the events in Warsaw, only the steady trembling of his uninjured right hand showing signs of life. But Himmler was too angry to notice the Führer's strange lack of interest. 'Führer,' he exclaimed, his sallow face flushed with rage, 'I know the moment is not opportune from a historical point of view. But what the Poles are doing is a blessing in disguise. Within five or six weeks, it will be all sorted out and then Warsaw, the capital, the head, the brains behind those sixteen to seventeen million Poles will be extinguished. That Folk which has blocked our way east for a hundred years, and hindered us since the First Battle of Tannenberg will no longer be a historical problem for us after this, or for our descendants.'

He licked the spittle away from the corner of his mouth and continued in the same excited tone. '*Mein Führer*, I want your permission to destroy Warsaw totally. I want to destroy each block of houses there so that the Polack rats can't dig themselves in. Our own staff people who will have to carry on there later won't like it. But no matter, let them learn what it's like to be a frontline soldier. I know those rear echelon swine don't like the sight of dead bodies.' He looked down at the ashen, trembling wreck of a man who controlled National Socialist Germany's destiny in this fifth year of war. '*Mein Führer*, what is your decision?' Hitler did not even look up. Without the slightest emphasis in his voice, he said huskily, 'Wipe them out.'

It was dark now. At the East Prussian Führer HQ, the 'Wolfs Lair', the orderlies were beginning to put up the blackout shutters and already the night patrols, twelve strong and accompanied by savage, half-wild Alsatian, were filtering through the resin-heavy pines searching for intruders. But in the stuffy tightness of Himmler's own HQ, every officer was at his desk. Telephones were ringing continually, and harassed clerks were running back and forth bearing the latest reports from the new Warsaw front.

Himmler, red-eyed and with dark shadows curving down the sides of his plump, unshaven face, faced the men who would be responsible for wiping out Warsaw. It was now four hours since he had first received the news of the Warsaw Uprising, but he still could not contain his rage. Pacing up and down the operations room, his grotesquely distorted shadow thrown on the wall by the flickering candles, he cried, 'I shall wipe Warsaw off the map. I shall destroy every one of them — man, woman or child! I shall raze their buildings to the ground. There won't be a stone left standing when I'm finished!' He stopped for breath, his skinny chest heaving with the effort, his nostrils flaring, white, manicured hands twitching convulsively behind his back.

'Reichsführer,' Obergruppenführer Berger, the cunning brains behind the SS, seized the chance to break into Himmler's tirade, 'what are your orders?'

Himmler spun round on the balls of his feet. 'You,' he pointed a forefinger at Berger almost menacingly, 'will ensure that every Polish political prisoner in our hands is shot by midnight. Begin with that Polish general — Rowecki — he's the brain behind these traitors. I shall expect a full list of all those executed by this time tomorrow. I want blood, Berger. *Blood*, do you understand?'

'It will be done, Reichsführer,' Berger answered, without turning a hair. He knew Himmler's rages. 'And the military measures?' Himmler directed his attention to the big SS general standing near the wall map of Poland, and studied him for a moment. General of the SS and Police, Erich von dem Bach-Zelewski, a big, burly shaven headed East Prussian, was the head of the SS Anti-Partisan Combat Units and an acknowledged expert in antiguerrilla warfare. Well-known for his loyalty to National Socialism and ruthlessness. In spite of his blind rage, Himmler knew instinctively that the East Prussian was exactly the right man for the task ahead.

'Bach-Zelewski, I want you to go to Cracow this night and take over the task of directing operations against those Polish traitors.'

'Reichsführer,' the General answered. 'What are my orders?'

'Raze Warsaw to the ground!'

Bach-Zelewski did not bat an eyelid at the prospect of exterminating a city of one million inhabitants. 'And what are the forces at my disposal, Reichsführer?'

'You will have overall command of all units presently fighting within Warsaw itself, and the relief force now being assembled by SS General Reinefarth at Cracow.'

'And they are?'

'Tell him, Obersturm Teufel,' Himmler said impatiently.

Bach-Zelewski turned and stared at the slim young SS officer with the dark un-German eyes and slanting cheekbones of a Mongol. Viktor Teufel flushed a little; he knew what the SS general was thinking. He, Teufel, did not look exactly like the ideal SS officer, the long-faced blond Nordic youth of the recruiting posters. 'General,' he said hurriedly, 'you will have at your disposal some eight thousand men, made up of Dirlewanger's Anti-Partisan Brigade and Kaminsky's Rona Brigade. Both will have attached self-propelled guns and a section of mobile flame throw —'

Bach-Zelewski held up his plump hand for the younger man to stop. 'But my dear Obersturmbannführer Teufel, Dirlewanger's Brigade is made up of ex-Soviet prisoners of war and jailbirds, who have volunteered for the front to escape death in the Homeland, and, if I am correctly informed, SS Brigadenführer Kaminsky's Rona Brigade is composed of Ukrainian collaborationists who haven't exactly gained the best reputation in their dealings with the civilian population over this last year.' He sighed. 'How am I supposed to capture a well-defended built-up area, against men who will undoubtedly fight to the death?'

'But they are exactly the types you need, Bach-Zelewski,' Himmler interjected hotly. 'Men who have nothing to lose and everything to gain. Men whose background show them to be completely ruthless, with none of our absurd German, sentimental reticence about taking the lives of women and children.'

'That may well be,' the big General persisted with the typical obstinacy of the East Prussian. 'But it is not only ruthlessness I will need if I am going to retake Warsaw. After all, one defender there will be worth three attackers — it's always the same when one is fighting in a built-up area. Such places can swallow up whole divisions — just like that.' He clicked his fingers together and Himmler started. 'I need experienced fighting troops.'

'The barrel has been scraped clean, Bach-Zelewski,' Himmler retorted. 'Since the Western Allies attacked in France, our resources have been strained to the limit. You will have to make do with what you call jailbirds and collaborationists.'

'Reichsführer.' It was Berger.

'Yes?',

'There *is* the Black Cossack Division south of Warsaw, still in reserve.'

'The Black Cossacks?' Bach-Zelewski queried.

Again Himmler turned to the dark, un-German SS Major. 'You tell him, Teufel. After all you were in at the start of the whole business. And you are my personal liaison officer with those Russian cowboys.'

Berger gave a faint laugh at the expression, but Himmler silenced him quickly with an angry look.

Swiftly Viktor Teufel explained how he and Peter von Kranz had rescued General Bogdan, a former Red Army officer who had been imprisoned during the 1938 purges, from Kazan Concentration Camp. The Cossack General had persuaded a large number of Cossack outlaws to join him in the trek westwards, to link up with the advancing German troops in the summer of 1942, where they had contributed greatly to the successful breakthrough of the German Army on the Caucasus front.

'But why do the Cossacks want to fight for us?' Bach-Zelewski asked when Teufel was finished with his explanation. 'They are not jailbirds like Dirlewanger's men, or renegades like Kaminsky's. They already had their freedom. Bogdan could have stayed in his mountains with the rest of the Cossack outlaws. From what you say, Teufel, they had been living there untouched by the Soviet authorities since the days of the Civil War. What had they to gain from joining us?'

Obersturmbannführer Teufel's dark Mongol face twisted into a sneer. 'Because, Herr General, I believe those fools of the Wehrmacht staff promised them they would be allowed to establish their own Cossack country in their old stamping grounds, once we had won the war, and they were naïve enough to believe the field greys.'

'As if the Führer would ever tolerate such a thing,' Himmler said contemptuously. 'Allowing the Slavic sub-human any form of independence — *unthinkable!*'

Bach-Zelewski was a fervent National Socialist, but he was also a soldier and an honest one. Now he stared at the Head of the SS in disbelief. How could one betray a whole nation like that, even in this moment of crisis? Berger flashed him a warning look and asked quickly, 'Well, General, do you want our Cossack cowboys, or don't you?'

'Yes, of course ... of course,' the big East Prussian replied, pulling himself together hurriedly. 'I'd be delighted to have them under my command for a tricky operation like this one.' Yet even as he said the words, he could not overcome his sense of revulsion, that he, too, an honourable German officer, was now to become party to the great confidence trick being played on the unsuspecting Black Cossacks.

'Good,' Himmler rapped, 'well that's done with. Bach-Zelewski, you have exactly forty-eight hours. I expect you to begin your operations against Warsaw on the morning of the Fourth. Clear?'

'Clear, Reichsführer.'

'And you Obersturm!'

'Yessir,' Teufel snapped, his face wooden and emotionless.

'You will take my personal *Storch* to General Bogdan's HQ this night and alert him about the new operation.'

'Sir! And your orders.'

'Just this, Teufel,' Himmler answered, turning towards him, a face hollowed out to a menacing skull in the flickering candlelight, 'I want his Cossacks to treat those Polish gutter rats like their forefathers did in the days of the Czar. In other words, rape, looting, murder. Anything goes. I want the Poles exterminated...'

CHAPTER 4

It was a beautiful summer morning. Soon it would be furnace hot again. Already the Polish plain quivered in the blue haze and in the village which had grown up around the Black Cossacks' camp, the brown wisps of breakfast smoke rose up from the little white house's straight into the cloudless blue sky. Everywhere the skinny-ribbed dogs lay in the shade, gasping open mouthed in the heat, and the heavy-set, barefoot, kerchiefed Polish women, who slept with the Cossacks, padded around slowly, every step requiring a fresh effort of will.

Far away to the north, the sound of gunfire came from the direction of Warsaw, but the Black Cossacks were hardly aware of it. It was the ever-present background music of war; they had heard it daily for three long years now. Slowly the few of them on duty went about their morning tasks, watering the still tired horses, throwing them bundles of hay at the end of their pitchforks, cursing and sweating with the heat as they began to brush the mud of the Vistula crossing from the animals' legs.

But mostly the Black Cossacks enjoyed their time out of war, backs to the walls of their huts, smoking their clay pipes, boasting of their exploits with their heavy-bosomed peasant mistresses while they bribed the tow-haired, ragged Polish boys with kopecks to fight furiously for them in the white dust.

General Bogdan and Baron Peter von Kranz, feeling that they had earned a morning off after the successful raid on the Red Army division, leaned against a fence and watched the General's bow-legged groom bring in the fine Trakehner mare, which this day would be mated with Bogdan's own stallion. Tossing away his long cigarette, Bogdan, minus his cap and coat, clambered over the fence and took the mare from the groom, who was grinning knowingly, his dark little eyes twinkling mischievously. 'Take that smile off your ugly mug, you rogue,' Bogdan said good humouredly, 'it's not you who's going to get it, you know.'

'How do you know I haven't already had it, Little Father?' the groom answered swiftly. 'You know what we Cossack farm lads are like.'

'Be off with you!' Bogdan cried and aimed a half-hearted kick at the grinning groom.

The man moved away quickly and the nervous mare twitched. Hastily Bogdan stroked her muzzle. For the last couple of days his own stallion *Don* had been paying the mare constant attention whenever he could, sniffing at her tail, nuzzling her neck tenderly, thrusting the mare's puzzled foal out of the way so that he could get closer to the mother. Now Bogdan attempted to calm the mare and prepare her for what was to come, giving an amused yet touched Peter von Kranz a running commentary as he did so. 'You see Peter, the Trakehner make the finest cavalry horses in the world. Your own General von Seydlitz discovered that a couple of centuries ago. But they're highly strung beasts, especially in season. Aren't you?' Tenderly he placed one big hand over the twitching mare's right nostril and breathed hard into the left one. The animal's nervousness ceased almost at once.

'In the old days, Peter, the Cossacks used to piss over the mare's muzzle. But breath does the same trick.'

Peter von Kranz shook his head in mock disbelief, as the mare's trembling stopped and a few metres away, the foal, bewildered by the whole business, bent its head and began to crop the yellow, parched grass.

Carefully Bogdan released his hold on the mare. Still she did not start. 'All right, you Cossack clod,' Bogdan commanded, 'you can bring in the clown now.'

'*Horoscho*, at your command, Little Father,' the bow-legged groom spat drily into the grass. 'What a life. Ugh! Always a couple of sniffs at it and never the real thing.'

Bogdan grinned at the little man's disgusted expression. 'If you'd have had more sniffs at it and less of the real thing, you might have had straighter legs, you rogue.'

'That comes from a lot of riding, General.'

'Yes, that's what I mean.'

The groom laughed uproariously and went to fetch the clown — a big ugly stallion, which was to test the mare's receptiveness for mating before *Don* was brought in to carry out the act.

'Jesus, Mary, Joseph,' one of the little barefoot Polish boys, who were watching the proceedings curiously, exclaimed, and crossed himself quickly in the Polish fashion, 'is that horse sick!' He pointed a dirty finger at the stallion's belly.

Bogdan laughed uproariously, tossing his black head back as he did so. 'If only I were *that* sick!' he cried.

Gingerly the groom led the excited stallion towards the mare. He held the halter loosely, ready to drop it and bolt if the mare acted up, as they often did on such occasions. But nothing happened. Tamely the mare accepted the stallion's attentions, as it nuzzled her tail, her body held perfectly still, her ears bent in submission. Bogdan nodded his approval. 'All right,' he called to the groom, 'she's ready. Otherwise she would have kicked all hell out of him. Take the clown away.'

The groom tugged at the reluctant stallion's bit. 'Come on, you poor old bastard. That's all *you're* going to get this day.' Sadly the big ugly horse allowed itself to be led away.

But Bogdan and Peter von Kranz were not fated to observe the final act of love-making, for at that moment they were startled by the roar of an aeroplane engine to the east, growing louder by the second. Hastily Peter von Kranz shaded his eyes against the glare of the sun. 'Fieseler Storch, General,' he cried above the noise. 'It's one of ours!... It looks as if we're getting visitors!'

'The Black Cossacks' time out of the war was over.

'Attack the Poles!' Bogdan exclaimed angrily and banged his fist down hard on the white scrubbed kitchen table, which served him as a desk, 'I have no quarrel with them, Obersturmbannführer!'

Viktor Teufel looked at the red-faced Cossack General out of the corner of his dark Mongol eyes. 'It is the Reichsführer's personal order.'

'You say that, as if you're speaking of God,' Bogdan sneered. '*Reichsführer*, do you think I'm afraid of your consumptive-faced Reichsführer!... We Cossacks did not leave our own earth to help you Fritzes repress other people. We left our country to fight for the freedom of our own people and defeat that monster Stalin. What are we otherwise?' He looked out of the window of the log hut at the corn-blond, cropped Polish boys scuffling happily in the dust. 'Mercenaries, renegades, that is what we would be. Hired killers who had betrayed their own country for thirty pieces of silver.'

The SS officer looked at the enraged, sweating General with a sneer on his dark face. 'What do you think you have been doing these —'

'*Obersturmbannführer, halt die Scheissschnauze!*' Peter cut him short with an angry burst of German. 'General,' he turned to Bogdan, speaking Russian again. 'You know that I have always supported your cause loyally these last two years. After all my family has always felt itself as much Russian as German. For two centuries the von Kranzs served the Czar loyally until the Communists put an end to all that.'

Bogdan nodded his head slowly, some of his anger vanishing. He knew and respected the one-armed blond German's sincerity. Peter von Kranz wanted to help him establish an independent Cossackia when Stalin was defeated. If any one of the Fritzes could get him back to his native Don, it was Peter. 'Yes, I know, little brother,' he said, the harshness gone from his voice. 'But how can we achieve our aims by attacking the Poles?'

'But isn't it obvious, General Bogdan, what the Poles are going to do?' Peter said persuasively. 'They are going to hand over Warsaw, lock, stock and barrel, to the Reds. With it, the whole German communications system for Central Poland — road and rail networks, airfields — will drop right into Rokossovsky's lap like a gift from the Gods. Then there will be nothing to stop the Red Army from advancing right up to the frontiers of the Reich itself. Our next natural line of defence would be the River Oder and you know what that would mean, General?' His voice was urgent as if he'd just realised the full import of his words himself.

'Yes, yes, I understand that, Peter,' Bogdan answered impatiently, 'but what has that got to do with us Cossacks? It is our Cossack homeland on the Don which concerns us.'

'I know, General,' von Kranz answered patiently. Viktor Teufel watched his efforts to pacify the big Cossack with contempt that a German officer would go to such lengths to explain to one of the Russian sub-humans. *A German ordered; he did not explain!* Hadn't the Reichsführer said that about the Slavs himself?

'But don't you see, General Bogdan,' Peter von Kranz was saying, 'the future of any Cossack state depends upon the success of German arms. This summer the Reich must buy time to perfect the revenge weapons which must bring us victory against the Red hordes this coming winter. Then you will be able to return to your Quiet Don and set up that state which the Wehrmacht High Command has promised you. The Poles,' he concluded urgently, 'are not patriots trying to overthrow German rule. Undoubtedly they are the bribed hirelings of Moscow who, now that the Red Army is on their doorstep, are prepared to hand over their country to the new masters. Forget the Germans. Those Poles in Warsaw are not only betraying us they are betraying their own people, believe me!'

Bogdan fell silent. Thoughtfully he sucked his teeth, half-listening to the cries of the little Polish boys outside. Two years before, Peter von Kranz, who had risked his life to free him from Soviet captivity, had persuaded him to throw in his lot with the Germans at Kazan Concentration Camp. Then he had searched his soul deeply too, wondering whether he should betray the Soviet Fatherland and throw in his lot with the enemy, for that was what the Fritzes were.

In 1942, he had told himself, he and his people, the Don Cossacks, had no homeland. They were historical ghosts, deprived of their lands by the Communists after the Civil War in which they had fought on the wrong side, the losing side. Like the Jews of old they had been scattered over the face of the earth, only a few surviving as outlaws in the inaccessible mountains of the Southern Caucasus.

Naturally, he had known, that the Don Cossacks had had a lot to answer for from the days when the Czar had employed them to put down the workers' revolts; when they had crushed any attempt to obtain liberty with their sabres and knouts. But he had thrown in his lot with the Reds right from the start as a young Cossack cavalry officer. Had he not fought against his own people in the Civil War and been disowned by his father because of it? Had he not led his regiment against the Poles in '20, fighting all the way to Warsaw itself before it had been decimated, guarding the rear of the fleeing Red Army? Had he not served Stalin loyally until that terrible day in 1938 when he had been publicly humiliated in front of his own division? That day his life had been destroyed.

After twenty years of loyal service to Soviet Russia he had been treated worse than a common criminal, thrown into prison without trial, not even allowed to see his wife and child. Two years later his beautiful Vera had been dead — a suicide according to the rumours he had heard in the concentration camp — while his son had vanished, probably into some Secret Police orphanage under an assumed name, where he would become a 'loyal' Soviet citizen.

Suddenly General Bogdan was overcome once more by a burning rage against the Soviet system which had destroyed him and his people; a rage he'd felt two years before when Peter von Kranz had first approached him in Kazan Concentration Camp. He slammed his big, sabre scarred fist down on the wooden table so that the vodka glasses trembled violently. 'All right, *Herr Baron*,' he cried, 'I shall fight the Poles for you in Warsaw. I shall play your German games one more time.' His fiery dark eyes flashed. 'But woe betide you Fritzes, if you lie to us again. The Cossack revenge will be terrible!'

CHAPTER 5

'They're a fine bunch of slit ears, General,' von Kranz whispered to Bogdan, as they waited in Bach-Zelewski's HQ. The harassed staff officers hurried back and forth, files under their arms, and the dispatch riders outside in the courtyard came and went in great flurries of white dust.

Bogdan nodded his agreement and looked across at Colonel Oskar Dirlewanger, the skinny, almost skeletal, Commander of the SS Penal Brigade. He knew the dark-haired decadent German's reputation. He was a pederast, who had been kicked out of the SS and imprisoned in a concentration camp for molesting a minor. But his protector, Berger, had wangled his release in 1940, and given him the command of the SS Penal Regiment: a two-thousand strong group of ex-concentration camp inmates, and ex-SS men, culled from the military prisons. Wherever the Dirlewanger mob made its appearance, there was wholesale looting, rape and murder. Even the SS had been horrified by their behaviour and only the year before, Berger had just saved Dirlewanger from the concentration camp again when Kruger, the senior SS and Police Commander in Cracow, had threatened to throw 'him and his bunch of criminals' into jail, if they weren't removed from the Cracow area within one week.

Now Dirlewanger leaned against the wall, smoking yet another cigarette in his ivory holder, drunk as usual, and trying to keep his soft hands off his sickly, handsome 'adjutant', who looked all of eighteen.

Across from him, surrounded by his SS officer bodyguard, Nicolas Kaminsky, CO of the Rona Brigade, stared at the big map of Warsaw, discussing the fighting in a quick mixture of Russian and German with his men, his gestures as swift and shrewd as his lean, sharp face.

Bogdan knew of him too. Thirty-five years old, of Polish-German parentage and fiercely anti-Soviet, he had formed his own brigade in the Ukraine, made up of local men and Ukrainian deserters from the Red Army. He was brought to Himmler's attention by Berger and within three months rose from being a humble village school teacher to an SS *Brigadenführer*.

At the end of 1942 he had conceived the idea of making a German republic of the Ukrainian province of Lokot, at that time overrun by Soviet partisans and other outlaws. By the start of 1944 Kaminsky's Rona Brigade had pulled it off: Lokot was cleared of all opposition and placed under German rule. Nicolas Kaminsky's name had become a byword for cruelty. Wherever he went with his Slavic SS men, he spread death and destruction, for as he proclaimed often enough to the civilians who were to come under his control: 'I don't ask you people to love me — *I want you to fear me!*' And they did.

'Are these the forces you Fritzes are going to use against Warsaw?'

Peter von Kranz nodded gloomily.

Kaminsky picked up the Russian and swung round in his quick, nervous way. 'Why do you ask, General Bogdan?' he asked in the same language. 'Do you not approve of us?'

Bogdan surveyed the undersized SS Commander for a moment. The man was a cunning opportunist, but brave in his way. He would fight to the end for whomever paid him to do so, but he would resort to the most underhand and cruellest means to ensure that he, Nicolas Kaminsky, was not the one who would die. 'No,' he said finally.

Kaminsky smiled thinly, but his calculating eyes remained cold. 'May I ask why, General Bogdan?' he asked softly.

Bogdan shrugged. 'If you wish. You are fighting for this,' He made the Russian gesture of counting money with his big thumb and forefinger. 'Men like you can change sides swiftly. The law of the highest bidder.'

Kaminsky flushed. Behind him his Ukrainian bodyguard tightened their grips on their Schmeissers; they had understood the insult in Russian well enough. 'That is a very unpleasant thing to say, General,' Kaminsky said, recovering himself quickly.

'I mean it,' Bogdan answered gruffly.

'But do you think you and your Cossacks are any different from my Ukrainians?'

Now it was Bogdan's turn to flush. 'What do you mean by that, man?' he barked.

Kaminsky smiled easily. 'Aren't we all the same underneath the blanket — renegades, serving a master, regarded as the enemy by our peoples? What is the difference between the Black Cossack Division and my Rona Brigade. You have sold your soul to the German too —'

He never finished the words. Beside himself with rage, Bogdan rushed forward. With one big paw, he lifted Kaminsky clean off his feet, his fingers biting cruelly into the SS Commander's skinny neck. A lieutenant lifted his Schmeisser. Bogdan kicked him effortlessly between the legs. The man screamed shrilly and went down, grabbing for his testicles. Dirlewanger took his hand off his lover and grabbed for his Walther. Peter took a step forward. For one moment, it looked as if the plan to relieve Warsaw might end there and then. But at that moment the door to the operations room was flung open and Bach-Zelewski bellowed in his harsh East Prussian voice. '*Aber, meine Herren, ich bitte Sie!*'

Slowly Bogdan lowered Kaminsky to the floor, while Bach-Zelewski stared at the scene aghast.

Kaminsky, crimson-faced and shaken, tugged at his tunic and whispered in a strained voice, full of hate, 'By God, Bogdan, you will pay for that, yes you will!'

Next to the General, Peter von Kranz shuddered involuntarily: the little SS Commander's dark eyes were full of a bottomless, intense hatred, and everyone knew that Brigadenführer Nicolas Kaminsky did not make idle threats.

Bach-Zelewski, visibly shaken by what he had just witnessed, stalked through the room to the big map, pushing Kaminsky's bodyguards aside, as if they didn't exist. 'Gentlemen,' he rapped, 'may I have your attention?'

The assembled officers turned in his direction.

'I am going to forget immediately what I have just seen. All I say is this — we'll have enough on our hands fighting the Poles, without wasting time fighting each other. Is that clear?'

'Clear,' those of the SS officers present, rapped.

'Good, now let us get down to business. Time is short.' The big East Prussian looked at the homosexual SS Colonel, hardly able to conceal his contempt. 'Dirlewanger, what is the state of your Brigade?'

'I have sixteen officers and nine hundred other ranks,' the Colonel replied in his soft, almost feminine voice.

'Not enough for the task I have in mind for you, Dirlewanger. Within the course of the next forty-eight hours, you will receive two thousand five hundred replacements. From the SS Military Prison at Matzlau near Danzig.'

'Thank you, General,' Dirlewanger said without enthusiasm, 'And my assignment?'

'You will approach the city from the east and begin your attack in the suburb of Kolo — here.' He tapped the map behind him. 'Your main axis will be along Wolska-Gorczewska Streets. You'll retake the Police Barracks if it's in Polish hands and push on to the Kercely Square. Understood?'

'Understood.' Dirlewanger's eyes flickered with interest as he followed the line of advance on the map. 'Looks a prosperous area. I should imagine there'll be plenty of loot there for my SS rogues.'

'Undoubtedly,' Bach-Zelewski commented drily. 'But remember, Dirlewanger, you are supposed to be conducting a military operation — and not a shopping tour without money,' he made the German gesture for stealing.

'I'll remember, sir,' Dirlewanger said and obviously pleased with his assignment, he smiled and placed his soft hand on that of his 'adjutant's'.

Bach-Zelewski looked away quickly. 'Kaminsky, what is the strength of your Rona?' he asked.

'Fully up to strength, General,' Kaminsky answered in that sharp, confident way of his, which had earned him Himmler's favour, although he was 'racially inferior', on account of his Polish mother. 'Ready for action as soon as you give the word, *sir*!'

The East Prussian General beamed. 'I'm glad to hear that. Good!' He looked at the sharp-faced Ukrainian in his simple uniform, devoid of any badges of rank or decoration save the Iron Cross, first class, to check whether Kaminsky was holding anything back. Satisfied that he wasn't apparently, he continued. 'This is what I want you to do, my dear Kaminsky. You will come in from the south-east, jumping off from the suburb of Okecie. Using your armour to cover your advance, you will attack along the axis of the Grojecka Street up towards the Narotowicz Square, with your prime objective the capture of the districts south of Wola on the insurgents' left flank. Is that clear?'

'Perfectly, sir,' Kaminsky answered at once, absorbing the information without the slightest difficulty, in his shrewd manner.

'Excellent. But you will have a secondary objective too.'

'It is, sir?'

Bach-Zelewski motioned him to be silent. 'Let me explain General Bogdan's task first.' He turned to the big glowering Cossack, still turning over Kaminsky's words in his mind. 'General Bogdan, you are in the command of my largest and most battle-experienced formation. It is only suitable, therefore, that you should have the most difficult and most militarily demanding objective. Translate please, Baron.'

Bogdan nodded, his resentment forgotten now, one hundred percent soldier. 'I agree, General,' he said at once, when von Kranz had finished putting Bach-Zelewski's words into Russian. 'What is it?'

'You will attack from the south towards Warsaw, through the Mokotow district, which Intelligence believes to be exceedingly well defended by the insurgents. You will then push into the old city itself and fight your way past the telephone exchange to your major objective — the relief of Marshal Stahel's HQ at the Bruehl Palace.'

Bach-Zelewski let the big Cossack General, a striking figure in his fur cap and black coat, absorb the initial information, then he said. 'As you can see from the map, you will have the Vistula on your right flank. Since both the Poniatowski and the Kierbetza Bridges are firmly in our hands, there will be no attack from that quarter.'

'And my left flank?' Bogdan queried when Peter had translated the General's words for him. 'I have a large area to cover and I won't be able to spare many men for a flank guard, General.'

'I know,' Bach-Zelewski replied hurriedly. 'Ah, but you'll have Kaminsky's Rona Brigade working its way forward parallel with you, won't you, Bogdan? I'm sure you can rely on Kaminsky to ensure that your left flank is covered satisfactorily. Can't he, Brigadenführer?'

'Naturally, General,' Kaminsky answered without the slightest hesitation, 'the General can rely on me.' He looked quickly at the glowering Cossack Commander and said in Russian. 'After all, we Ukrainians and you Cossacks are brothers under the skin. We're all in the same boat.' He smiled maliciously.

'Good, then that's settled,' Bach-Zelewski snapped. 'Any questions?' There were none. Each of the three commanders, one and all outcasts and renegades, were suddenly preoccupied with their own dark thoughts. For a few moments Bach-Zelewski stared at the widely divergent officers: one a pervert, the other a merciless renegade killer, the third a professional soldier, forced by circumstances to raise his hand against the very men he had served with for over twenty years, and he wondered what was going on in their minds at that particular moment. Then he pulled himself together.

'Gentlemen,' he announced in his harsh East Prussian voice, 'you have exactly twenty-four hours. We march on Warsaw at precisely zero four hundred hours on the morning of fourth August. *Heil Hitler!*'

'*Heil Hitler!*'

BOOK TWO: *THE FIRST ATTACK*

'When we've dealt with the Cossacks, we'll ensure that Brigadenführer Kaminsky receives the fate he deserves. But first we kill General Alexei Bogdan.'

General Bor to General Pelczynski, August, 1944.

CHAPTER 1

The dawn sky was still, silent, broken only by the odd trickle of blue smoke from the little houses to the Cossacks' front.

It all looked very peaceful, but Bogdan, crouching next to Peter von Kranz in a ditch at the side of the little country road, was aware that each of those houses was held by determined men, who would kill without hesitation. Soon there would be nothing peaceful about this August 4th dawn.

Next to him von Kranz glanced at his wristwatch.

'Well?' Bogdan queried and flung a glance at his young Cossacks lying flat on the ground all around them, hands tensed on their weapons.

'Any minute now, General,' the one-armed German answered. Behind them Viktor Teufel crouched lower in the ditch, anticipating what was to come.

The minutes passed leadenly. The sky began to flush a first red. Suddenly they were there: a swarm of bent wing hawks, stark black in the sun.

'The Stukas!' Peter said excitedly. 'Dead on time.' Bogdan turned on his back and stared up at the German dive-bombers. They were long outdated, easy meat for any fighter. But the Poles had no fighters and no antiaircraft weapons. The ugly dive-bombers would be able to attack with the same impunity they had enjoyed in 1939, when they had first shattered the Polish capital. 'Stand by!' he yelled above the noise of their engines, as the Stuka leader waggled his crooked wings in recognition of the swastika flags and big arrows they had spread out on the grass in front of their positions. 'They're going in!' The Cossacks rose to their knees. They would rush the Polish positions as soon as the Stukas had done their deadly work, before the Polish defenders had a chance to recover.

Now the Stukas were directly above the houses. For a moment they seemed to hang there in the blood-red sky, like a group of hawks. Abruptly the leader jiggled his wings, once, twice, three times. It was the signal. Without warning, he dropped out of the sky. At 500 kph, sirens howling crazily, the Stuka leader hurtled towards the ground. Behind him plane after plane peeled off and did the same. Suddenly the sky echoed and re-echoed with their ear-splitting roar, as the planes sped to seeming destruction.

Just as it appeared inevitable that the Stuka leader would crash headlong into the houses, he levelled off, motors screaming in frantic protest, and the whole plane trembling madly with the almost unbearable strain. A clutch of wobbling black eggs fled from the plane's belly. Plane after plane pulled up in mid-air and discharged its bombs. For one long instant, there was a dead silence, broken only by the thin whine of the bombs speeding to their target below.

Abruptly the world erupted in one great crazy roar. The ground trembled beneath Bogdan's knees. Automatically he clutched at the sack of Don earth round his neck. A wave of hot, acrid air slapped him in the face. He gasped for breath fervently and closed his eyes.

When he opened them again, their whole front was one long continuous line of blazing houses, a high wall of scarlet fire, roaring and darting flames, with black smoke pouring skywards. A frightful panorama of death and destruction.

But General Bogdan had no eyes for the terrible, awesome beauty of the scene. As the Stukas fled the way they had come, as if desperate to escape the site of their merciless slaughter, he rose to his feet and yelled, 'Black Cossack Division — *forward!*'

Crazily his young soldiers scrambled up and ran into the smoke, screaming: '*Vperjodi ze osvoboshdenije rodini!*' 'Forward to the Freedom of the Homeland!' Bogdan bit his lip at the words of the old Cossack war cry. Would they achieve their freedom by destroying the freedom of another people? Then he, too, was caught up by the heady excitement of the attack. Swinging his sabre above his head, his staff following him, he stormed after the others into the swirling cloud of smoke, yelling: '*Vperjodi ze osvoboshdenije rodini!*'

The attack on the suburb of Mokotow had begun!

They fought all that burningly hot morning. The Polish first line was taken without difficulty. The Cossacks swarmed through the enemy positions before the dazed, bleeding defenders were aware of what was happening. A group of the Cossacks, made overconfident by that first easy victory, pushed ahead of the rest of the Division to be trapped in a narrow side street by a bunch of Colonel Daniel's *Kanalarki*. Using their special knowledge of the capital's sewer system they had hidden from the bombardment and come up behind the Cossack front. The fanatical Polish youths shot the Cossacks down without mercy. In the end the handful of survivors cried in a mixture of Russian and broken Polish, '*Tovarsch* — *we surrender ... surrender!*'

'Throw away your weapons and come forward with your hands in the air!' the blond eighteen year old commander of the *Kanalarki* section ordered, his captured German *Schmeisser* machine pistol levelled at the bleeding, terrified Cossacks.

Obediently, unsuspectingly, the Cossacks came forward, young faces terribly pale, hands raised high in the air, and halted in front of the *Kanalarki* positions.

The Pole looked at them contemptuously. 'You are Russians — Slavs — yet you fight against your brothers!' he accused.

'We were ordered to,' one of the Cossacks quavered fearfully.

'*Ordered to*!' the boy bellowed, beside himself with rage, the veins sticking out at his temples and throat. '*Yes, by the Fritzes, eh?*'

He rapped something to his companions in Polish. A couple of the boys, who stank of the sewers, darted forward. 'Boots off!' they commanded harshly.

Unaware of what was going to happen to them, the Cossacks pulled off their good German boots and flung them to the waiting *Kanalarki*, many of whom wore shabby rubber soled tennis shoes.

'On your knees!' the boys ordered next.

It began to dawn on the Cossack prisoners what was going to happen to them. 'No ... no!' they pleaded, holding up their clasped hands to their captors in the classic pose of supplication, their faces contorted with fear. '*Mercy...*'

But the fanatical young *Kanalarki* had no mercy. They kicked their prisoners into submission. Like dumb animals, the kneeling Cossacks waited while their executioner went from man to man, placed the muzzle of his pistol behind his right ear, and blew him into eternity.

Finally the slaughter was over, and their bodies, frenetic from their violent death, sprawled in the white dust of the street.

Tonelessly the *Kanalarki* leader ordered: 'Bring me paint and a brush!'

When they were found, the *Kanalarki* commander himself seized the brush and began to paint one word on the first of the dead Cossack's foreheads...

'*Traitor!*' the Cossack patrol leader breathed the word and tore his gaze from the dead man's glassy eyes, already covered with the flies which were now everywhere, 'they've painted the word "traitor" on his forehead.'

Stiffly he rose to his feet and stared at the rest of the patrol. 'What does it mean?'

'I'll tell you what it means, you young greenhorn,' a wrinkled Cossack, his tunic heavy with the medals of the Old War, exclaimed angrily. 'Those Polish whoresons have murdered our boys in cold blood after they surrendered! Look at the back of their heads. Murdered! *Shot from behind!*'

'*Shot from behind... The Poles are shooting prisoners from behind...*' The word went from mouth to mouth as the Cossacks pushed forward that blazing afternoon, under a merciless red-hot sun, with terrible effect. Regardless of their losses, they stormed a Polish strongpoint at the Woronicz School, and slit the throats of the wounded as they lay among the worn school benches, carved with names of generations of school children. The severely wounded commander of the defenders was carried half-conscious to the great cross that dominated the school hall, and in the Cossack fashion was nailed to it — *upside-down*!

The atrocities had commenced.

Later that afternoon, while Boris set about cleaning up the battle littered school for use as the Black Cossack Division HQ, the lead elements of the Division assaulted the Elzbietanek Hospital. It fell without much fighting. The handful of downcast dirty prisoners were lined up against the hospital's bullet pocked wall and machine gunned. Then someone shouted enthusiastically. 'There's women here, boys!'

'*Women*!' the hoarse cry went up on all sides.

Oblivious of General Bogdan's explicit order to keep advancing at all costs while Colonel Daniel's Poles were still retreating before the Division, the excited young Cossacks swarmed into the hospital, crunching over the broken glass and debris, screaming the old Cossack cry: '*Fornicate and be merry, lads!*'

A burly Polish woman in the uniform of a chief nurse tried to bar their way, her arms outstretched like a schoolmarm trying to restrain a bunch of excited children. Half a dozen crazily laughing Cossacks seized her. In an instant she was stripped naked, her hands trying to hide her pendulous, massive breasts, as a dozen hands fumbled frantically with her body. When they were finished with her, she lay on the floor, a great heap of bloody twitching flesh, which shuddered every time a fresh Cossack boot sank into her body.

They barrelled into the nurses' quarters, crashing the door down. The nurses screamed with fear. An old bearded Cossack grabbed the nearest girl with a loud whoop of glee and thrust his dirty hand up her skirt. 'Come on, my Polish pigeon,' he cried happily. 'Let me show you how a Cossack makes love!' He pressed his bearded face against hers ignoring her puny fists which pummelled his broad chest helplessly.

The Cossacks yelled with joy. One of them seized a nurse and swinging her clean off her feet, threw her on the nearest bed. The mass rape of the Elzbietanek Hospital's teenage nurses went on.

General Bogdan and his staff rode into the debris littered courtyard of the Hospital, just as the rapists had begun to swarm into the wards, screaming and drunk on looted medical alcohol, in search of fresh victims. He took in the situation at once. With Boris and von Kranz on both sides of him, pistols drawn, he waded into the drunken mob of Cossacks, lashing out with his knout on all sides, bellowing at the dazed youths to get back to their sections.

A drunken captain, naked save for his fur cap and boots, staggered towards them down the centre of the ward, a bottle of medical alcohol in one hand, a half-conscious girl clasped in his big hairy arm.

'Captain!' Bogdan commanded. 'Let go of that child!'

In his drunken stupor, the officer did not realise that he was speaking with the feared Alexei Bogdan. '*Tuoya mat!*' he mumbled the gross Russian obscenity through slack, wet lips, and attempted to move forward.

Bogdan did not hesitate. 'Boris,' he ordered. '*Fire!*' The Chief of Staff pressed the trigger of his German Luger. The pistol leapt in his hand. The first slug caught the drunken, naked Captain in the belly. Suddenly his tight white stomach was flushed a dark red. The second caught him in the shoulder and slammed him against the wall.

'But General,' he cried, staring at Bogdan with horror-stricken, pain-filled eyes, as he realised abruptly to whom he had spoken, 'what —'

The third bullet struck him directly in the face. The girl screamed as the Captain's head disappeared in a mess of bright red blood and broken bone. Slowly his body slithered down the wall, leaving a trail of red behind it.

Bogdan ignored the dead man. 'See to her, Peter,' he indicated the swaying girl and strode imperiously towards the group of rapists, who fell back on both sides, their eyes wide with sudden fear. 'By the Holy Virgin of Kazan, I'm going to have discipline in my Division!' he roared and brought his clenched fist across the face of the nearest soldier. The man reeled back, his cheek flushed a dull purple. 'What do you think we are — barbarians?' Bogdan cried, beside himself with rage, his face a bright scarlet. 'We are here to fight Polish men, not to fornicate with Polish women! My God, I'd like to shoot each and every one of you mean bastards!' He swallowed hard and tried to control his overwhelming anger.

'General, I thank you, on behalf of the Polish people.' The voice was feminine, controlled and educated, speaking Russian with only a trace of a Polish accent.

Bogdan spun round. A dark-eyed woman stood there at the door of the next room, the mask of a surgeon dangling from her neck, her body swathed in the shapeless white rubber apron, spotted with bloodstains. But it could not quite hide the beauty of her figure. He took in the woman's generous mouth, the bold eyes, the wisp of white-gold hair escaping from beneath the white cap and asked sharply: 'Who are you woman?'

'My name is Roswitha Jankowski — *Countess* Roswitha Jankowski. An out-worn title.'

Bogdan ignored the comment. Behind him the Cossacks were bearing the dead captain's body away and the girl was beginning to sob. 'What are you doing here?' he demanded harshly.

'Let me show you, General.' She crooked a gloved finger at him and automatically he followed her into the next room.

It was filled with wounded men, lying limply on the blood-soaked stretchers like dolls from which the sawdust had run out. On the operating table under the blue white glare of the high-power lamps, a young soldier, his face like clay, lay with his legs drawn up in the embryo position. With a start Bogdan recognised the uniform. 'It's one of my Cossacks,' he exclaimed.

'Yes,' the woman said softly. 'One of the men who attacked us. But for us it makes no difference — German, Russian, Pole, you are all men needing my help,' She laughed suddenly. It was a strange sound to hear in that dreadful place of death. 'So that you can fight again and die a glorious death such as that for your country,' She pointed at a Polish boy from Daniel's Command, dying in the corner, his intestines pulsating in front of him on the blood-red floor like an obscene pale-grey worm at every shallow breath. 'Like that!'

Bogdan did not hesitate. He turned to Boris. 'Major, ensure that the hospital is evacuated at once!'

'General!'

'And put an armed guard round the place immediately. A twenty-four hour guard,' He slapped his knout against the side of his high riding boot. 'There will be no more rape or shooting of prisoners in the Black Cossack Division as long as I, Alexei Bogdan, command it…'

That same night General Alexei Bogdan and Senior Surgeon Countess Roswitha Jankowski became lovers. As General Bor had planned they would three days earlier!

CHAPTER 2

Brigadenführer Nicholas Kaminski had no such scruples as General Bogdan that terrible August day. As the blood-red sun began to sink beneath the pall of smoke which hung over the Wola suburb, his propaganda company's vehicles started to crawl through the conquered streets. '*Achtung, Achtung,*' the loudspeakers blared in German, '*alles herhoeren!*' And then in fluent Polish, for there were enough Polish renegades too in the Rona Brigade, 'circumstances have forced the Command of the 29th SS Division to order the evacuation of this quarter. Follow the instructions given you by the soldiers of this command and nothing will happen to you. Brigadenführer Kaminsky gives you his personal assurance that you will be rehoused in adequate quarters and given sufficient food. *Do not take food with you!* Just your most valuable possessions. You have exactly five minutes before our attack recommences. '*Achtung... Achtung, alles herhoeren!*' the tremendous overwhelming voice echoed and re-echoed in the tight stone walls of the narrow streets.

As the strident, harshly metallic note of the loudspeakers died away, the civilians, grateful that they were being given this chance to escape from the embattled quarter, began to stream from their houses. They clutched their most valuable possessions, those things which might buy them some sort of a future — jewels, gold watches, a handful of precious silver coins, a single rare stamp.

Kaminsky's Ukrainians were waiting for them. Their smoking weapons were slung over their shoulders and they were smiling and helpful, not the grim merciless SS killers the

Polish civilians had anticipated. They aided old women to adjust their hastily thrown together bundles; they picked up the dolls and toys dropped by the wide-eyed children; they joked politely with the younger women, their eyes already counting the rings on their fingers. Like lambs being led to slaughter, the civilians formed up in long columns and followed their butchers obediently to the west.

For nearly half an hour the long column wound its way out of Wola until it came to the area of the cemeteries, where for three centuries the people of Warsaw had buried their dead. Now the SS men, lining both sides of the debris littered street, were no longer smiling, nor so helpful. When the old women fell, they were booted into the dirty gutter and their valuables torn from their nerveless fingers to be distributed hastily among the greedy, hard-eyed SS men.

The Polish civilians started to hunch together. Their chatter died away and their eyes no longer dared meet those of the field-grey shapes standing on both sides of the road which led to eternity.

Suddenly an armoured car of the Rona Brigade cut in from a side road and the column came to a ragged halt. Brigadenführer Nicolas Kaminsky himself, stood upright in it, loudhailer clasped in his well-manicured, pale hand. For a moment he stood there, infinitely menacing, staring at the awed, frightened civilians in silence. He pressed the catch. The loudhailer came to life with a crackle of electricity. 'Dogs of Poles!' the great echoing voice boomed out, 'drop your bundles! At once, you traitors!'

The column hesitated. A Spandau hissed into violent, frightening life. Red-hot tracer whizzed suddenly over the civilians' heads. Panic-stricken they dropped their bundles, as ordered. 'Good ... good,' Kaminsky cried over the loudhailer.

'At last you Warsaw rabble are learning some sense! Now then — all of you — move to the left. Towards the cemetery! *MARCH!*'

Frightened, faces blanched, already sensing what was going to happen to them, the civilians turned to the left and began to move into the waiting machine guns. The Rona SS men did not hesitate. It wasn't the first time that they had 'cleared' an area of enemy civilians. The massed guns opened fire at point-blank range. The civilians, screaming and howling with fear, went down by the score. Panic-stricken, those behind tried to clamber over the twitching bodies to escape, only to run into the deadly hail themselves. A mother, shot through the breast, let go of the pram she was pushing. The carriage began to roll down the incline, the baby shrieking wildly. A Ukrainian, his broad Slavic face set in a huge grin, pulled the china pin out of his stick grenade and lobbed it easily at the pram. It exploded in a thick burst of purple flame. When the smoke cleared, all that was left was one solitary bent wheel wobbling crazily down the incline.

And still the massacre went on, while further up the road, other Ukrainians looted the civilians' possessions, giving cries of joy whenever they came across anything particularly valuable. A man attempting to use the wall of dead to cover his escape, was caught as he emerged into the open again. For a few moments the grinning, sweating gunners played with him, firing bursts in front of him and behind. The man darted back and forth like a crazy monkey, screaming with terror as the vicious bursts of fire struck up a pattern of blue sparks on the cobbles. Then tired of their game, the gunners deliberately took aim and ripped his body apart with one long burst.

Finally Kaminsky, standing aloof, every inch the great commander on the turret of his armoured car, had had enough.

'Cease fire … cease fire!' he bellowed through his loudhailer. 'You've wasted enough ammunition on those Polish swine now. *Cease fire!*'

The firing petered away and there was an echoing silence, broken only by the piteous whimpering of the wounded. Someone in the bloody mess of dead and dying civilians, piled up like logs of wood in front of the smoking Spandau's, kept crying 'Mama, Mama', over and over again, 'help me!'

But there was no help forthcoming for the handful of survivors of the massacre. Pitilessly the hard blue sky looked down on the last terrible act of that afternoon at Wola, as the Ukrainians started to spill petrol over the bodies. A few moments later one of them threw a phosphorous grenade into them. In an instant the huge funeral pyre burst into violent flame. As the flames engulfed them, those of the civilians who had feigned death or who had been unconscious, tried to escape. Clothes afire, babbling incoherently, the demented creatures would attempt to crawl away from the all-consuming flames. But the Ukrainians had no mercy and fired swift bursts at the would-be escaper, forcing him back into the flames to crawl around in crazy circles, seeking escape as the flames leapt higher and higher, until he collapsed, his burning head in a pool of petrol.

Coolly Brigadenführer Kaminsky watched the terrible scene until the obscenely sweet stench of burning flesh became too much even for him. Clasping his manicured hand over his beaklike nose, he rapped to his adjutant: 'Signal Reichsführer Himmler direct! *Suburb of Wola completely cleared of partisans. Heil Hitler! Kaminsky.*' He grinned suddenly. 'Now let's get at those Polish whores you found me!'

The adjutant grinned and clicked his heels together in a fair imitation of a regular German officer. '*Zu befehl, Brigadenführer!*'

In high good humour Kaminsky strode off.

'Oh, my God,' General Bor groaned above the rattle of the German machine gun across the way, 'it can't be true, Pelczynski!'

Glumly his Chief of Staff nodded. 'It is, General. One of our *Kanalarki* watched the whole barbaric business. He's downstairs if you wish to talk to him.'

Bor fought back his tears. In spite of his dour appearance, the stern mien of a professional soldier, he was an emotional man. 'No, I don't want to see him, Pelczynski. I believe the scout. I've heard of that swine Kaminsky. Wasn't he the bastard who cleared Minsk last year?'

'The same, sir.'

Bor fell silent for a moment. Outside the German slugs careened off the tobacco factory's thick walls with frightening regularity. So far the uprising had gone off surprisingly well. Most of the old city was under his command, save Stahel's HQ. Soon he hoped to take the Vistula bridges by storm, and open the way for the Red Army to advance into the city; then, having defeated the Germans, he would be in a position of strength to deal with the Reds when they marched in. But now he saw the danger that faced him now from Bach-Zelewski's push from the east and south-east.

'Look at this, Pelczyn,' he said, turning to the big map of Warsaw spread out on the table. 'You can see what the Fritzes are attempting to do, can't you? They are obviously trying to cut us in half, by thrusting up into the old city.'

His Chief of Staff nodded agreement. 'Yes, but I don't think we've got too much to fear from that direction, sir. Our people are well dug in and even if they manage to break through our first line, the strongpoints of the Police Barracks and Telephone Exchange will hold them up easily.'

'Agreed. My main fear is here.' Bor stabbed his finger at the map. 'The Mokotow district. Those Cossacks are experienced, well trained soldiers. If they succeed in their push, they can crush us against the Vistula. With those bridges still in German hands, we'll have hardly any room to manoeuvre.'

The Chief of Staff's grey face grew very serious in the white glare of the hissing carbide lantern. 'Of course, I see the danger. But what do you suggest we do, General. Our resources are limited.'

'What have you in reserve, Pelczynski?' Bor snapped, making up his mind abruptly.

'The Kedyw-Radoslaw Assault Group.'

'Excellent, they're all good men, ideally suited for the task I have in mind.'

'And that is, sir?'

'From our source with the Cossacks, I have learnt that they've set up their headquarters at the Woronicz School — here. Now I want the Assault Group to wipe that HQ out in a raid. Without this General Bogdan of theirs, the Black Cossacks are not much more than a rabble. Those who fought against them in '20 know how they go to pieces without officers to keep them in check.'

'Admittedly, sir,' the Chief of Staff said hastily. 'But the Kedyw-Radoslaw Assault Group would have to penetrate a good four kilometres into the Fritz lines and they'd be constantly threatened by the possibility of a flank attack from Kaminsky's bandits from the Wola district.'

'So?' Bor said calmly.

His Chief of Staff looked at his superior in bewilderment. 'I don't understand, sir.'

Bor made the Polish gesture of counting money with his thumb and forefinger. 'Isn't that the only thing that a cut-throat like Kaminsky understands, Pelczynski?'

'You mean bribe him, sir?' the Chief of Staff gasped.

'Certainly. Pay the disgusting wretch to look the other way when our people go through the lines. It's been done before, hasn't it? Didn't the Hungarian Division offer to sell us their heavy weapons the day before yesterday if we could pay for them in British pounds or American dollars? Believe me, Kaminsky can be bought ... and then when we've dealt with the Cossacks, we'll ensure that Brigadenführer Kaminsky receives the fate he deserves.' He hesitated momentarily, his face hard and set in the hissing white glare. 'But first, Pelczynski, we kill General Alexei Bogdan...'

CHAPTER 3

'*Are they ready?*' Garbaty, the Commander of the attack squad breathed, as the mechanics fumbled with the looted German devices in the darkness of the hedge. A couple of hundred metres away the blacked out Woronicz School, which was now the Cossacks' HQ, was shrouded in silence, broken only by the steady rumble of gunfire behind them in Warsaw.

'Only a few moments more, Commandant,' the senior mechanic whispered urgently, as he checked that the remote-control wires were securely attached to the deadly little monsters.

'Good, good,' Garbaty answered. 'Take your time, but ensure that nothing goes wrong.'

Garbaty turned his attention to the NCOs once more. The bribe had worked. Kaminsky's Ukrainians had looked the other way as they'd sneaked across no-man's land two hours before. To Garbaty, barely able to conceal his hatred of Ukrainians and yet suspicious of their motives, it had seemed as if they almost welcomed the Polish penetration of their front; as if they knew what his intentions were and approved of them. Now they were grouped within striking distance of the enemy HQ, and the enemy had obviously not spotted them. In a matter of minutes they could unleash their attack, with every prospect of complete success. 'Now this is the plan. We'll split into two sections of twenty men each. I'll command the one on the left, you, Joseph, will take the right one.'

'Yes, Commandant,' the burly, dark-haired NCO answered smartly, as if he were a Regular Army NCO and not a former lady's underwear salesman up to last week.

'When I give the word, we'll crawl forward and take up our positions. You Joseph in that clump of shattered trees over there … I'll take that outhouse at ten o'clock,' He grinned in spite of his inner tension. 'With my luck, it'll probably be the school's thunderboxes — and they won't have been emptied for the last five years.'

The others chuckled softly.

Garbaty turned to the mechanics. 'When we're there, I'll whistle. That will be the signal for you to get your nasty little toys moving. And don't let me down or I'll have the eggs off you with a blunt cut-throat.'

'Don't worry, Commandant,' the senior mechanic answered, wiping the sweat off his forehead with the sleeve of his greasy overall, 'we won't.'

'What are they, Commandant?' Joseph asked, expressing the bewilderment of the rest of the assault squad, who had taken turns towing the two tarpaulin-covered objects on a cart, for four kilometres behind the Fritz lines.

'The Goliath,' Garbaty announced solemnly. 'Another of those nasty little devices the Fritzes keep dreaming up to kill their fellow human beings in ever increasing numbers. They're still on the secret list, but we managed to nab a couple of dozen of them two days ago when we captured the SS depot. They're a kind of mini-tank, controlled by those wires the mechanics are fixing to it —'

'You mean remote-controlled?' Joseph interrupted.

'Yes. The senior mechanic here can steer them to their target, hidden from the bottom of that ditch there, without any risk to his dirty mechanic's hide. Two hundred pounds of high explosive moving forward at fifteen kilometres an hour, impervious to small arms fire or hand grenades. And if even the Cossacks had antitank guns up there in the school, they'd have a devil of a job stopping the Goliath, since it's only sixty centimetres high — a hell of a target for a normal gun to hit,' He reached forward and patted the nearest of the two mini-monsters with his big, hard hand. 'This time, lads, Goliath is going to knock the shit out of David. All right, let's get on with it. And remember once those Goliaths have knocked down the school walls, in you go with the bayonet,' he fixed them with his eyes, his face a glowing death's head in the flickering red light over Warsaw, 'and don't forget, that big bastard of a Cossack General must not escape…'

In spite of his weariness after a murderous day of commanding operations at the Mokotow front, Bogdan could not sleep. His mind still raced with the details of the plan of attack he would put into operation on the morrow; and the room, closed in on all sides by the blackout curtains, was as sweltering as a Cossack village bakehouse. With an angry groan at his inability to sleep, he opened his eyes and stared at the dim, white outline of the naked woman's body sprawled out on the sheet beside him. He ran his big calloused hand across the damp skin of Roswitha Jankowski's breasts. She sighed softly and her big dun nipples grew hard and erect. He made the same gesture again, but she did not open her eyes.

Bogdan gave up. She had worked all day in the hospital, operating for twelve solid hours on both Polish and Cossack wounded, her rubber boots soaked in blood, severed limbs on the floor all around her. Then they had made love until the small hours of the morning, moaning and groaning with savage, animal pleasure till she dropped off into a gentle, satiated sleep. Now it wouldn't be fair to wake her. Bogdan grinned and told himself he was getting old. As a young man, he would not have bothered about such things: a Cossack took what he wanted, where and when he wanted it, without worrying what the wench felt.

Careful not to disturb her, he rose from the bed and tugged on his boots. He would have a smoke outside — perhaps the cigarette would calm his nerves and enable him to sleep.

But he was not alone in his inability to sleep. Peter von Kranz, clad solely in his breeches and white, collarless shirt was standing near the shattered main entrance to the school, smoking a cigarette and staring pensively at the burning sky above Warsaw. 'You, too, Peter?' Bogdan said softly and waved for him to carry on smoking.

'Too sultry inside, General — and then, I don't know,' the one-armed German shrugged a little irritably, 'I've got an uneasy feeling.'

'What kind of an uneasy feeling?'

'I can't really say,' the German answered hesitantly. 'But before I turned in, I had a last look at the situation report. The map shows a thousand metre gap between us and the Kaminsky Brigade. That's a pretty big hole, General. Think of von Kluck in '14!'

Bogdan chuckled. 'This is not the Marne and the Poles are not the French and English. Now they are on the defensive — they won't attack against regular troops. Why should they? They can achieve much more by remaining on the defensive. We saw that again today,' he added grimly. 'Besides, that slit ear Kaminsky is covering our flank.'

'I suppose you're right, General,' Peter von Kranz answered and puffed hard at his cigarette, but his voice was without conviction.

'It's just nerves, Peter, battlefield nerves. It happens to all of us, even a Bogdan. Besides this kind of battle isn't for me, nor you, I'll wager. Give me a fight against regular troops any day, however tough. I don't like having to fight against civilians. It's...' he sought for the right word '...too messy.' Peter von Kranz looked at the big General out of the corner of his eye, as Bogdan stared a little helplessly at the flames above the beleaguered Polish capital, and guessed what was going through his head. He told himself it was always wrong to take a mistress, especially one as beautiful and sympathetic as the Countess Jankowski, from an enemy people. It was better to resort to the whores, as he did, whose only loyalty was to the money with which one bought their favours. Then one didn't get unnecessarily involved.

'What do you think our chances are of breaking through to Stahel in the next forty-eight hours, General?' he asked, trying to change the subject.

'Pretty good, Peter. The Poles will make us pay — heavily — for every metre of ground we gain in the built-up area, but tomorrow after the feint attack goes in, I shall personally direct—'

He stopped short suddenly. 'What was that?' he demanded, his hand dropping to the big pistol buried in the waistband of his breeches.

'What was what?'

'Over there — to the right.'

Peter von Kranz cocked his head to one side and heard it too — a strange whirring sound reminiscent of the electric trams of Petersburg in his boyhood. For a long moment he stood there, transfixed, bewildered, completely unable to identify the source of the sound. Then he spotted it: the squat metallic slug crawling purposefully towards the schoolhouse.

'What in three devils' name is it, Peter?' Bogdan gasped, staring at the object emerging from the gloom, which looked for all the world like the clockwork tank he once gave his son on his name's day in another world.

'*A Goliath*!' Peter rapped. 'One of the new weapons our people have dreamed up, to be used against fieldworks, bunkers, strongpoints and the like.'

'How?'

'It's a remote-controlled explosive device. Two hundred pounds of high explosive with a range of a thousand metres.'

'*What*?' Bogdan exploded. 'Then by sweet Jesus's name, the Poles have —' He broke off, suddenly galvanised into action. Raising his pistol in the air, he pressed the trigger. The shot shattered the stillness of the night. '*Alarm ... alarm*' he bellowed at the top of his tremendous voice, '*Stand to — the Poles are attacking*!'

As the startled Cossacks woke, stumbling out of the schoolhouse, and blinking in the sudden darkness, as they fumbled for their weapons, there was an angry command in Polish to their front. A ragged but effective volley of Polish fire stopped the leading Cossacks dead, as if they had run into a brick wall. Abruptly the headlong rush into the gardens halted. The survivors retreated back into the schoolhouse. There was the sound of felt blackout curtains being ripped away and window glass smashed with rifle butts.

Crouched at the back of the house, Bogdan groaned. 'Don't bog down!' he cried aloud 'For God's sake, don't bog down or we're sitting ducks!'

But already it was too late. There was a sudden stab of scarlet flame from the window directly above him as the Cossacks began to return their attackers' fire from within the schoolhouse itself.

Now there was no time to consider the Cossacks' reaction. The monstrous little tank was getting ever closer. Bogdan took careful aim with his pistol and fired. The slug struck the front of the Goliath. A spurt of blue flame and the bullet went whining off into the darkness. 'Shit!' Bogdan cursed.

'It's no use, General,' Peter called as the Goliath continued its relentless progress towards the house.

'What?'

'They're proof against small arms fire.'

'How can we stop the bastard then, Peter?'

'There's the control wires!'

'Where are they?'

'At the back, General. That's the only way to stop it! They link up with the fellow controlling its movements.' With his one hand, Peter gestured wildly towards the bushes five hundred metres away. 'My guess is that he'll be hiding out there somewhere.'

Bogdan made a decision. 'Come on, Peter, let's see if we can give it the kick up the arse!' Crouched low the two officers doubled forward towards the Goliath. The Poles spotted them at once. Slugs hissed through the air.

Bogdan cursed and stumbled.

'Hit, General?' Peter gasped.

'Shit no,' Bogdan cried, recovering himself. 'A scratch. Come on!'

They ran on. A Polish egg grenade hurtled over their heads and missed. Red hot steel shards hissed by them frighteningly. But luck was on their side; they were not hit. Together they hurtled over a rickety fence. The Poles were firing all out now; perhaps they had guessed the two running men's intention. Bogdan could hear the slugs careening off the little tank, advancing upon them with uncanny inhuman determination. Bogdan doubled to the side of the Goliath. This way he was protected from the Polish fire. Peter did the same. Bullets pattered against the Goliath's side like heavy summer rain, as they kept pace with it, trying to assess the problem facing them.

'Where are the wires?' Bogdan gasped.

'To the rear!' Peter cried, his breath coming in harsh gasps.

Bogdan stopped in his tracks. 'Wait till it passes,' he commanded, 'and grab the shitty things! *NOW*!'

Together they dived for the cables which trailed behind the Goliath like the twin smears left by a slug. A sudden lather of sweat broke out on Peter's forehead. What if the operator had spotted them too, and exploded the charge now? There wouldn't be much left of them if he did. The wires began to tighten and he had no more time to consider that frightening possibility. It was now or never.

The sudden strain on their hands was terrific. Peter felt his single palm begin to burn almost unbearably with the wire. His fingers were on fire. 'Pull, Peter!' Bogdan groaned through clenched teeth and gave a mighty heave as the German did the same.

Nothing happened. Somewhere in the red darkness, a voice shouted a command in Polish. Was it to blow the tank up? The Goliath ploughed on across the gardens with eerie inexorability. Peter fell to his knees. The ground grazed his flesh cruelly, as the Goliath dragged him forward. Next to him Bogdan dug in his heels, as if he were back in the stables, trying to hold onto a stubborn unbroken horse. 'Hold on, Peter!' he called desperately. 'Hold on...' He, too, went down on his knees. *'Come on, you bitch, won't you ever —'*

Suddenly he fell backwards, as the wire came away in his big bleeding hands and the Goliath came to an abrupt stop, the soft whirr of machinery silent.

'We've done it, sir!' Peter yelled with joy.

Bogdan, squatting in the dirt, beamed across at him in the darkness. 'My Christ, you're —'

The tremendous explosion as the other Goliath struck the far end of the schoolhouse drowned the rest of Bogdan's words. A huge hot wave of blast slapped him almost physically across his surprised face. Gasping frantically for breath, his head ringing wildly, his lungs threatening to burst at any moment, the General staggered to his feet. There was no time for self-congratulation now. There was work to be done. 'Come on, Peter,' he choked, 'the Polish buggers are already attacking the main entrance!'

With desperate courage the Poles attacked again and again. Twice they got as far as the main entrance hall, throwing grenades in front of them, like deadly black snowballs, and swaying back and forth in hand-to-hand combat under the disapproving gaze of the high-collared bewhiskered nineteenth-century worthies who stared down at them from the bullet pocked walls. And twice they were driven back.

They tried a third time, but they had now lost the initial surprise element and the entrance hall defences were still intact. Thus, as the first ugly white of the false dawn began to fill the sky and the sound of horses' hooves came ever nearer at a furious gallop, they gave up and began to pull back into the woods from which they came. They left the main entrance littered with the pathetic young bodies of their dead and their dying commander, a great hole torn in his guts, lying on the steps.

CHAPTER 4

'I'm afraid, I can't help him anymore, General,' Roswitha said slowly, letting the bloody swab in her hand fall to the floor helplessly. The Polish countess was still dressed only in a white silk petticoat and as she bent over the harshly gasping Polish leader, the contours of her generous, bed warm body were clearly visible through the thin material.

But the staff officers grouped round the dying AK man had no eyes for Roswitha's beautiful body; their gaze was fixed on the young Pole, his ripped open stomach packed with cotton swabs, like white eggs laid in a scarlet nest.

'Roswitha,' Bogdan said carefully, as the cavalry clattered to a halt outside, 'ask him how he managed to get so far behind our lines like that without being discovered, and how he knew where my HQ was?'

She hesitated and looked at him, almost in reproach.

'Please,' he added with surprising gentleness for him and touched her arm for a moment.

She nodded and bending closer to the dying youth, asked her question in Polish. His eyes flickered open, closed and then opened again. He looked up at the woman bending over him, his eyes liquid with pain. Then the haze cleared and he saw that well-remembered face. A new light came into his eyes. But before he spoke to her, he saw the hated grey uniform all around her and the light died again almost as soon as it had come.

'Ask the swine again!' Teufel ordered angrily, perhaps the only one of the group peering down at the youth, who had seen that look of what seemed to be recognition in his eyes.

'He's dying, you know,' Roswitha said tonelessly.

'Ask him again, please,' Bogdan urged. 'It is highly important for us to know. And then we can let the poor fellow die in peace. Otherwise —' he left the sentence unfinished and glanced briefly at Teufel's dark Mongol face.

Roswitha followed the direction of his gaze and her beautiful face paled. She understood. Teufel would not hesitate to torture Garbaty, if he didn't talk. She bent down over him again. 'Tell them what you know,' she said softly, piercing him with her dark eyes, forcing him to understand, willing him to make the right reply that would protect her and make for trouble between the various factions in the enemy camp.

Garbaty understood. He craned his head forward. Slowly his parched, bloodless lips formed the word, 'Ka … min … sky…' Then his head fell back and he was dead. Her eyes full of tears, Roswitha Jankowski reached out her hand and gently pressed down the lids of the dead youth's eyes. 'For Poland,' the words formed soundlessly on her lips. '*For Poland!*'

'That bastard Kaminsky — I knew it!' Bogdan roared and crashed his big fist down on the table rattling the breakfast coffee cups.

Boris, Peter and Teufel stared at his crimson, enraged face, but said nothing. Outside the HQ, Cossacks were carrying away the dead like sacks of potatoes, while others, stripped to the waist, sweated in the morning sun, filling sandbags to pack the gap in the wall made by the Goliath.

'But can you trust a Polack's word?' Teufel broke the silence suddenly, a sneer on his thin face.

'Why not?' Bogdan snapped, preoccupied with his own dark thoughts. 'The man was dying. What had he to lose?'

'There might have been someone else behind it,' Teufel persisted. 'Perhaps he was trying to protect somebody, eh?'

Bogdan did not seem to hear. 'That murderous Ukrainian bandit would do anything for money. Everybody knows that. Look what he did the other day at Wola. That piece of mule dung would sell his own whore of a mother if there were enough money in it! ' he concluded angrily.

'But what can you do about it, General?' Peter von Kranz protested. 'Even if your assumption is true — and personally I believe it is. *Grosse Kacke am Christbaum*, the man deserves to be behind prison bars! I know the Ninth Army would like to get rid of him immediately. And I don't think General Bach-Zelewski would object either if Kaminsky disappeared from the scene. The man has become a devil of a burden for the German High Command.' Peter looked at Teufel hastily. 'But he has powerful friends at court who will excuse any of his misdeeds.'

Teufel flushed. 'Are you referring to the — Reichsführer SS?' He said the words, as if they were in italics.

Peter ignored the comment. 'Besides, General, Kaminsky has surrounded himself with a bodyguard of thugs who never leave his side. They're only loyal to him. After all he pays them well enough with loot to ensure it.'

'There are other ways,' Bogdan said darkly. 'We can play Kaminsky's kind of games too, you know, comrades.'

'What do you mean, General?' Peter asked.

'Kaminsky's treachery has cost me twenty good men wounded and ten killed. I refuse to continue the fight here in Warsaw with a rotten, treacherous bastard supposedly guarding my flank and leaving it open every time the Poles grease his dirty palm with gold. By God, no! First get rid of Kaminsky and then we continue the battle.'

'But General Bogdan,' Teufel protested, 'Kaminsky enjoys the full confidence of the Reichsführer as von Kranz has just stated.'

'I don't care if he enjoys the confidence of God himself,' Bogdan answered angrily, 'I'm going to reckon up with the bastard.'

'All right, General, we understand,' Peter von Kranz said quickly, not giving Teufel a chance to interfere again. 'A lot of us would like to get rid of Kaminsky. But it is my guess that the Rona Brigade would refuse to fight if they suspected anything well — er — improper had happened to their commander. If they're loyal to anything at all, it is to their commander.' He licked his dry lips. 'And Bach-Zelewski needs the Rona to beat the Poles.'

Bogdan grinned suddenly, the plan already beginning to form in his mind. 'Yes, yes,' he said hurriedly, 'I understand. So we must arrange that Brigadenführer Nicolas Kaminsky meets with an unfortunate ... er ... accident, mustn't we?'

CHAPTER 5

Brigadenführer Kaminsky was in high good humour as Peter von Kranz and Viktor Teufel marched up the aisle of the shattered, looted chapel in which he had set up his headquarters. He sat on the altar, his booted legs dangling, drinking Polish vodka from a gold mass goblet. Around him, his officer bodyguard, hung with grenades, ammunition, and looted Polish pistols thrust into their belts, lolled in the ancient pews. They smoked and drank vodka straight from the bottle, their camouflaged helmets tipped to the back of their shaven flat Ukrainian heads.

The two German officers came to a halt in front of the altar. Idly Kaminsky continued to drink. Finally the Rona Brigade Commander deigned to notice the presence of the two officers, who stood to attention under the suspicious gaze of the surly louts who made up his bodyguard. Cruelly he tweaked the girl's nipple relinquishing his hold, as she yelped with pain. 'Well?' he demanded, 'what do you two Christmas tree soldiers want from me?'

They clicked their heels together and reported in the German fashion: '*Oberstleutnant Baron von Kranz und Obersturmbannführer Teufel melden sich gehorsamst zur Stelle!*'

Kaminsky's piggish little eyes narrowed! 'A baron and an obersturmbannführer, eh!' The ex-village schoolmaster, who in only eighteen months had become an SS colonel with the ear of Himmler himself, was very susceptible to flattery (as Bogdan had guessed). Now he was obviously impressed. 'And what is the occasion for such an honour, gentlemen?' he asked in his Ukrainian-accented German.

'Brigadenführer Kaminsky,' Peter snapped, 'we are from the headquarters of the Reserve Army —'

'Himmler?' Kaminsky broke in.

'Yes, sir,' Teufel said hesitantly, not enjoying the role he was being forced to play by Bogdan. 'We have a message for you from the Reichsführer.'

Kaminsky thrust out his skinny hand, laden with looted rings. 'Give!' he commanded.

Teufel, who hated anything Slav, flushed at receiving an order from a racially inferior Ukrainian. Nevertheless he reached in his cuff and brought out the letter. Kaminsky grabbed it eagerly — he knew how much he owed Himmler, the ex-chicken farmer, now head of the million strong Black Guards of the SS. Swiftly his little eyes took in the instruction on the cover, 'To be Transmitted by Officer Courier Only' and realised that its contents must be important. He tore the envelope open and quickly took in the message:

'My dear Kaminsky,

It gives me the greatest pleasure to inform you that in recognition of your outstanding services to the German cause, our Leader Adolf Hitler has seen fit to award you the Knight's Cross of the Iron Cross. Accordingly you will attend my Headquarters at Cracow this evening, 8th August 1944 to receive the decoration from my own hand. With comradely greeting. Heil Hitler!

Yours Heinrich Himmler'

Kaminsky looked up at the two of them, his eyes gleaming excitedly. 'Do you know the contents of this letter, gentlemen?' he asked.

'Yes, sir,' Peter von Kranz answered, trying to control the excited thumping of his heart. He was swallowing the bait! 'We are to escort you to the Reichsführer's HQ personally to receive the award.'

Kaminsky nodded and rapped an order in Ukrainian to his bodyguard. They started to stir themselves, and the drunken girl pouted as she realised that her lover was leaving her.

Peter and Viktor had understood the order; Ukrainian was little different from the Russian they both spoke as well as their native German. But they pretended surprise as the bodyguard began to assemble in the littered aisle. 'Are these officers to go with us, too, sir?' Peter asked.

Kaminsky nodded, buttoning up the neck of his grey tunic. 'They are my bodyguard and one can't be too careful. Those Polish swine of partisans are everywhere.'

'Agreed, sir,' Peter said. 'But we've only a short distance to go to the plane.'

'The plane?' Kaminsky's eyes lit up again.

'Yes, sir,' Teufel snapped. 'The Reichsführer has sent his personal *Storch* to fetch you. He didn't want you risking your life on the roads at this time of the day. Even though Wola Park's not more than a kilometre from here.'

'That is a different matter.' Kaminsky turned to the bodyguard. 'All right, I won't want you for the rest of the night,' he ordered in their native language. 'You can stay here, get drunk, whore, do what you like.'

The heavily-armed thugs slumped down in the pews and Peter von Kranz breathed a sigh of relief. The first stage of the murder plan had succeeded.

The grey, camouflaged Mercedes swung round the corner of the shell holed road, narrowly avoided the usual pothole and almost ran over the man waving the red signal lamp. The Ukrainian driver cursed and braked just in time. 'What the matter?' he cried in broken German, sticking his head angrily out of the side window. Behind in the rear seat, squeezed in between von Kranz and Teufel, Kaminsky grabbed for his pistol.

Then everything happened very quickly. There was a rush of grey-clad figures from all sides. Torches blazed into the interior to illuminate the driver's terrified eyes and Kaminsky's bewildered face, as he recognised the uniforms as German. '*What?*' the driver gasped and fumbled for his pistol. A club hit him over the head and he slumped across the wheel. A pair of brawny arms dragged him out and dumped him on the road. Peter and Teufel grabbed hold of Kaminsky. He struggled furiously, guessing already that he had been betrayed, lashing out with his arms and legs, with the fury of a man who knew that this was his last chance to escape death.

But the two Germans were too much for him. He was bundled outside, bleeding from a wound in his forehead, his cap pushed absurdly to the back of his head.

'Hurry, we haven't much time,' Bogdan's voice hissed from the bushes at the side of the road.

'*You!*' Kaminsky gasped, ceasing his struggles, when he saw the huge, black-clad figure of the Cossack General, fur cap set at a rakish angle, long Russian cigarette in the corner of his broad mouth.

'Yes, Brigadenführer. I, Alexei Bogdan,' The Cossack General raised his knout and slashed it mercilessly across Kaminsky's narrow face.

The Brigadenführer reeled back, a scarlet weal burning across his white cheek. 'What does that mean?' he cried, in terror and bewilderment. 'We are comrades-in-arms!'

'*Comrades-in-arms!*' Bogdan spat contemptuously. 'You treacherous little rat of a pen-pusher! You lie in your teeth!' He raised his knout again, but Peter von Kranz caught his arm just in time.

'No more marks, General. Remember the plan!'

Bogdan let the knout fall from his scarred wrist, while Kaminsky's little black eyes flashed from face to face, trying to read something there in the gloom. 'What do you mean?' he stuttered. 'What plan?'

But no one answered. Now everything was controlled haste.

They knew they were in the Rona Brigade area. A patrol could stumble across them at any moment. They had to carry out the plan swiftly.

While Teufel and von Kranz guarded a sobbing, broken Kaminsky with their pistols, Cossacks started to smear blood from a dead goose across the back seat of the Mercedes. A group of others opened the back of the waiting truck and began to unload the dead bodies of two Poles, who had been killed at the attack on the schoolhouse. A moment later they were draped dramatically in the ditch, rifles forced into lifeless hands, as if they'd been shot while attacking the car. Boris wrapped his pistol in a bundle of rags, and stepping up to the Mercedes, shattered its windscreen with one shot. 'The driver!' he rapped.

Quickly a couple of the Cossacks dragged the driver back into his seat and laid him with his head over the wheel. Carefully Boris aimed his pistol. There was a thick muffled crump. The driver's body jerked convulsively, and his head shattered into a thousand pieces, flinging great gobs of blood all over the interior of the big staff car.

For a moment there was no sound, save Kaminsky's sobbing and the steady throb-throb of the car's motor. Boris stuffed the scorched rags into his tunic. 'General,' he broke the silence, 'we're ready now.'

Bogdan took out his pistol. Softly he clicked off the safety catch. Kaminsky heard the sound. He looked up, his runtish face stained with tears, and saw the pistol. 'What's this?' he breathed, knowing already that his last moment had come.

'If you were another man, I'd give you a chance to say a last prayer,' Bogdan said quietly. 'But all your life, Kaminsky, you've worshipped the devil. You don't deserve such a chance.'

'You're not going to shoot me?' Kaminsky croaked, raising his thin pale hands, as if to ward off the steel bullets.

Bogdan ignored the question. He nodded to Peter and Viktor Teufel to move out of the way.

They moved rapidly. Kaminsky, his face contorted with terror now, saw the movement. 'No ... no,' he cried, his voice high and hysterical, '*no, not that*!' He started to move backwards, hands held out in front of him, tears streaming down his face, mumbling incoherently to himself. Bogdan raised his pistol, Kaminsky was five metres away now. There was a heavy electric tension in the air. All eyes were fixed hypnotically on the two men: the traitor and his executioner.

Suddenly Kaminsky swung round and began to run. It was the moment that Bogdan had been waiting for. As he pressed the trigger, scarlet flame spurted from his pistol. The slug caught the running man in the small of the back, and he flung up his hands dramatically. For a moment he faltered, then dragged himself on. Bogdan fired again. Kaminsky gave one last scream and slumped to the ground face down.

For what seemed an age, no one moved. Then Boris darted forward, pistol at the ready. But there was no need for the coup de grâce. Standing up again and dusting his dirty knees, he said: 'General, the devil's dead at last.'

Bogdan crossed himself in the Russian fashion, then glancing around the scene of the ambush, he ordered in a strangely toneless voice, 'All right, back to the trucks... We've still got a battle to fight in Warsaw...'

Minutes later they had disappeared into the night, leaving their victims to stiffen, while the motor continued to tick over steadily, in the darkness.

BOOK THREE: *THE BETRAYAL*

'I am not prepared to help a group of criminals who have embarked on the Warsaw adventure in order to seize power, exploiting the good faith of the inhabitants of Warsaw, throwing almost unarmed people against the German guns.'

Marshal Stalin to Winston Churchill 2nd September, 1944.

CHAPTER 1

General Bor woke up on the morning of August 14th, 1944 with an uneasy feeling he could not place. He lay on the floor of the factory, watching the first light filter through the shell holes in the factory wall and listening to the steady thump-thump of Mark IV's cannon, which had been shelling the old tobacco factory for two days now. Suddenly he identified his unease. The Soviet artillery which had been rumbling for weeks now on the other side of the Vistula had stopped firing!

He sat up and listened more carefully. His ears had not deceived him. The Reds had ceased firing. Angrily donning his boots, he stepped carefully over the exhausted young men who littered the floor everywhere, and went into his operations room, once the factory's washroom.

Pelczynski was already there rubbing his unshaven face with a damp cloth: it was two days now since the Germans had cut off their water. 'Well, General?' he said. 'You've heard it, I presume?'

Bor wiped the back of his hand over his scummed, cracked lips. 'Yes, I've heard. The bastards have stopped attacking, and you know what that means?'

His Chief of Staff nodded grimly. 'They're going to let us die.'

'Right! They'll allow the Fritzes to wipe us out and then they'll attack again. Once they've captured Warsaw they'll put their own puppets in power. But by God, Pelczynski, I'm not going to give them that pleasure! When they enter Warsaw, they'll find loyal Poles waiting for them — Poles who are loyal to the London Government and want a free Poland.'

'I understand, General,' Pelczynski said, lowering his voice so that the two radio operators on duty could not hear. 'But how are we going to do it?'

'With Kaminsky gone, the steam has gone out of the Fritz attack in the west. Our only real threat is that Cossack bastard Bogdan in the south, but as soon as the Fritzes realise that the Reds are no longer attacking, they'll pull out troops from the frontline and counterattack towards the bridges. Once they've linked up with their people holding the bridges, they'll undoubtedly launch an all-out attack on all fronts. We won't be able to withstand an attack of that kind with the forces available to us. We're stretched too far.'

'You're suggesting a shortening of our front, General?'

'Correct, Pelczynski. We'll withdraw to the old city, maintain a loosely linked series of strongpoints — with our main forces underground.'

'The sewers?'

'Yes, the place is riddled with them. We can move our people from strongpoint to strongpoint as the need arises, with impunity. Our *Kanalarki* know the sewers like the back of their hands. We'll make the Fritzes pay in blood — a lot of blood — for every metre of ground they gain, and by God,' he crashed his fist on the table in a rare exhibition of fury, 'we'll still be here when those Bolshevik bastards finally deign to attack again!'

That morning Bor and his staff went underground. At eleven o'clock they descended into the main sewer which led into the old city. The stink hit them in the face with an almost physical impact. Bor blanched and looked at Pelczynski. His face was as pale as death and his eyes were filled with horror at the prospect before them, the dark maw of the metre-high tunnel, its floor covered with an indescribable, sluggishly flowing, green mess, which shuddered frighteningly every time a German shell struck the ground above. With difficulty Bor pulled himself together and said hoarsely to their teenage guide, who had been handing each of them two crudely-shaped, short sticks, 'Your instructions?'

'Gentlemen,' the boy's voice echoed and re-echoed down the tunnel, magnified and distorted by the vast speaking tube of a sewer, 'for those of you who haven't been down the sewers before, the first rule to obey is not to panic. There is nothing to fear if you keep your heads and follow your guide. But you must watch your footing! Underneath the shit — excuse me General Bor?' the boy's face coloured hotly.

'Get on with it, lad, I know what shit is all right.'

'Thank you, sir. Well, as I was saying, underneath this mess there is broken glass everywhere. If you fall and cut yourselves, there is a very good chance you'll get septicaemia. So don't fall. That's point one. Point two. You'll find the deeper we get into the system, the hotter and stuffier the air will get. The mess at our feet generates a devil of a lot of heat. But don't worry, there is enough oxygen everywhere to keep going. Every hundred metres, I'll stop under an airhole, wherever possible, so that you can get some fresh air.'

'And the sticks?' Bor queried, looking down at the sticks the boy had handed him.

Their guide grinned. 'Well, sir, I'm afraid you'll have to learn how to play kangaroo again like children do.'

'How do you mean?'

'This, sir. Here, we're in a collector sewer, and we can get through it relatively easily. But some of the link sewers are much smaller and then this is the only way to move.' He bent forward until he was almost doubled up, his whole weight supported by the two small sticks, looking like an old man suffering from acute arthritis. Painfully he twisted his head round, and attempted to grin. He failed badly; the strain was too much. 'When we're in this position,' he continued, 'we play kangaroo like kids.' He made a short awkward jump forward and then once again. 'It's slow, exhausting, and painful progress, gentlemen,' he said, standing up once more with a sigh of relief. 'But it's better than a Fritz bullet any day.'

Bor nodded silently, doubtful whether a Fritz bullet were not preferable to what lay before them.

'Good, gentlemen, if you're all ready,' their guide said cheerfully, 'I suggest we start wading through the — er — shit,' A few seconds later Bor and his staff had disappeared into the frightening, pitch-black darkness.

It was a monstrous journey; their every groan magnified to a lion's roar and a German shell striking the road above their heads, shaking the dark tunnel in a way which stretched their taut nerves to the very limit. At times they waded up to their waists in the hot stinking mess, fighting every metre of the way, with heaving chests and frantically gasping breath. At other times, they hopped forward on the short sticks like overgrown schoolboys. Metre after metre, until their limbs were on fire and their backs about to break from strain.

After what seemed an age, they bumped into the first dead body, which blocked the whole centre of the passage. 'Body!' their guide called, 'we're getting close now,' He clambered over the body, as if he were crawling over a rock. When his turn came, Bor shuddered, as his hand struck the man's stomach. The corpse gave a soft sigh, as if it were still alive, his nostrils were assailed by a fetid stench from the long dead man. Hastily he turned his head away, retching drily, as he fought back the bitter green bile which had flooded his throat.

They crawled on. Bor felt himself sinking into a state of quiet dementia. The bodies became more frequent and their youthful guide took this as a good sign. 'We can't be far off now,' he kept calling back over his shoulder, his voice echoing and re-echoing down the tunnel. 'Not much further now, gentlemen!'

But still there was no sign of the exit. The gas generated by the hot mire beneath their feet began to affect Bor's eyes. He felt as if coarse sand lodged beneath his eyelids, and his head was rolling uncontrollably from side to side. Time and time again, he attempted to pull himself together, cursing himself angrily under his breath. But a few moments later his head had begun to gyrate again. 'My God,' he prayed fervently, 'let it end now!'

One of the radio operators slipped into the hideous bubbling mass. Before anyone could do anything, he had disappeared from sight, the only sign of his presence a hand still clawing frantically for a non-existent hold.

'*Oh God in heaven*,' Pelczynski behind him croaked, '*won't this ever end*!' Then as if in answer to Pelczynski's desperate prayer, their hot, sweat-lathered faces were struck by a gust of cool air. A happy voice shouted from above. 'Dworkowa Street — all change here. *Terminus*!'

Bor recognised the cry; it was the one used by the old city's tram conductors. At that moment it seemed to him the most beautiful words he had ever heard in his life. 'Thank God,' he breathed harshly, as strong hands reached down and began to drag him up from the clinging mire, which released him reluctantly. Their nightmarish journey was over. They had reached the old city.

Two hours later, Bor was established in his new HQ. While his boots dried in the corner, and his jacket was soaked with cheap cologne to drown the nauseating stink of the sewer, he dictated the first of his pleas for aid to the Allies. 'I categorically demand help in ammunition and antitank weapons forthwith, and on the ensuing days. A struggle lasting several days at least awaits us and we must be supplied throughout that time. We have staked everything on holding the capital. As DZ I suggest the Jewish Cemetery, Napoleon Square or the Little Ghetto. Our ability to hold out now depends on receiving ammunition from you.'

Bor listened carefully as the clerk read the message back to him. Outside there was the first inhuman cough, followed by an obscene sigh which indicated the new HQ was due for a mortar barrage. 'Good,' he said approvingly, raising his voice above the new noise, 'send it as it is.'

'But to whom should I address it?' the pale-faced clerk answered, the paper shaking in his thin hand as the first bomb landing fifty metres away shook the house violently with its impact.

'Churchill, of course,' Bor answered. 'If any one of three of them — Roosevelt, Churchill or Stalin — is going to help us here in Warsaw, it will be the Englishman, mark my words.'

A moment later the full weight of the mortar barrage had descended upon the old city and General Bor realised instinctively that the Fritzes knew of his move, and the fact that he had shortened his front. The battle for the old city could commence. Now everything depended upon Churchill resupplying him before Bogdan's Cossacks and the Fritzes on the other side of the Vistula, launched a co-ordinated attack on his new positions. It was a race against time. As the HQ rocked crazily with explosion after explosion, General Bor fought for control. *Would the fat Englishman in far-off London pull it off?*

CHAPTER 2

The whole line trembled like a dying animal, and the earth shuddered under the weight of the German bombardment. Again and again the mortar bombs crashed into the Polish positions, their angry red trails streaking after them as they fell out of the sky above Warsaw.

Now it was furnace hot. The glare cut the eyes of the watchers like the blade of a knife. Above the waiting Cossacks crowded into the silent side streets, the sun shone through the sultry sky, like a dull copper coin.

But in spite of the terrible heat, the Cossacks were ready. All day long Dirlewanger's criminals had been battering the new Polish positions in the Old City, on their left flank. As soon as the barrage ceased they would go in at the gallop, hoping to catch the Poles off guard. The Bruehl Palace, which was Marshal Stahel's HQ, was only five hundred metres away. If they could break through to it by storm and reach the defenders, they would have cut the Polish defences in half and have pressed them up against the River Vistula. Then it would only be a matter of time and organisation, before General Bach-Zelewski launched a two-front offensive which would completely break the Poles' obstinate resistance.

Now the mortar barrage started to slacken off. They could make out the sound of small arms fire again as the Poles popped up from their holes and sewers and began shooting at Dirlewanger's ex-convicts. Bogdan, at the head of the lead squadron, knew the time to attack had come. He raised himself in his saddle and swung his sabre around his head twice. It flashed boldly in the rays of the copper-coloured sun.

'Cossacks,' he bellowed above the noise of the dying mortar bombardment, 'prepare to march!'

One hundred metres away, Wanda, sprawled on top of the flat-roofed shattered store, heard the command faintly. She could not make out the words, but she understood what it meant. 'OK, my little pigeons, the sticks will be coming soon!' she warned. Her 'pigeons', twenty youthful snipers of both sexes, settled themselves more comfortably in their hiding places and waited for their 'sticks': their victims. Draped in dust-coloured cloths, their faces painted dull grey, the metal parts of their rifles darkened with grease, they looked for all the world like another pile of rubble, as they waited on the roof to spring their trap on the unsuspecting Cossacks. Sweating under her camouflage, Wanda Chochim, who in another age had been a nun, started to say the 'Hail Mary'. But her frail, pale hands were not clasped in prayer; they were clasped around the butt of her telescopic sniper's rifle!

Cautiously the Cossack scouts trotted down the sides of the shattered street, sabres drawn, the sound of their horses hooves echoing hollowly in the hot, sterile stone canyon. Even the most unfeeling of them sensed the eerie atmosphere of the place, and the rear men in each troop turned time and time again in their saddles to peer behind them. But there was nothing there. Just the empty, shattered scenery of war. It seemed that General Bogdan's attack was going to come as a complete surprise to the Poles.

They halted in front of a pathetic barricade, made of household possessions — chairs, sofas, even a child's pram — dragged hurriedly from the nearest houses and piled up in a futile attempt to stop the enemy. The captain in charge of the scouts issued a swift order. A couple of sweating, red-faced

Cossacks slipped from the gleaming backs of their mounts and began to clear away the barricade; as the ex-nun had planned they should do.

She raised her rifle, and brought the captain into the round, calibrated sight. *For a Cossack,* she thought, *he had a pleasant, sensitive face, pale and withdrawn; not the heavily-moustached, lecherous, brick-red features of the Cossack of the legends.* She told herself hurriedly, not to think of him as a man, but as a 'stick'. Gently her finger curled round the trigger and began to squeeze it with an even, steady pressure. Around her, her 'pigeons' did the same. The time had come to spring their trap.

The single rifle shot shattered the silence of the hot, oppressive street with the impact of a 75mm cannon. The captain threw up his hands. His fur cap slipped down over his face and soundlessly he dropped from his horse and slapped on to the cobbles. 'What in three devils' name!' a bearded old Cossack next to him cried, and attempted to bend down over the captain's body. At once, a slug caught him in the small of the back, smashing him against the wall with tremendous force.

An instant later the massacre began.

First the pigeons took out the NCOs. They fell from their horses with great shouts which abruptly died in their throats. The Cossacks, completely panicked now, wheeled and turned their rearing horses whose nostrils flared in terror. Desperate to escape that terrible trap, they trampled the bodies of the dead, fighting their way through the dying horses, struggling to rise, their slack mouths bubbling with pink-tinged foam. But there was no escape. With cruel, mechanical precision, Wanda's pigeons pumped one well-aimed shot after another into the panic-stricken, grey-clad soldiers below. Cossack after Cossack hurtled to the ground in sprawling death, or tried to crawl away on all fours to be executed by a sniper's bullet before he had gone a metre.

In the end, only one old, white-whiskered Cossack escaped the trap. Already bleeding from three wounds, he allowed himself to slump down onto his saddle as if dying. The snipers lifted their fire from him. It was the chance he had been waiting for. His body pressed hard against the right flank of his sweat lathered horse so that its body protected his from the enemy fire, he tugged at the bit cruelly. The horse whinnied frantically and lurched forward at the gallop.

'*Stop that stick*!' Wanda cried angrily and fired a wild shot, which missed.

Another pigeon fired. The big, black horse staggered. Bright red blood jetted from its flank. Desperately the old Cossack jerked at the bit. The horse found its feet again and bolted forward. A moment later, it had disappeared from sight around the nearest corner, leaving behind the dead bodies of thirty Cossacks, sprawled out in the rubble of the street.

'The roofs are full of them … snipers … dozens of them!' the old Cossack gasped, his back against the bullet pocked wall, his tunic ripped open to reveal his bloody, heaving chest. 'We didn't have a chance. They killed the captain and then —'

Gently Bogdan placed his big hand on the old man's gleaming forehead. 'All right, little Father,' he said softly. 'That's enough. You've done your bit. Rest and let the medics work on you now.'

'Shit, General, there are only a few scratches! Let me get at those Polish murderers.' He spat a gob of red tinged spittle onto the ground and tried to raise himself. He failed miserably and the battalion surgeon moved forward with the morphia hypodermic.

'You'd think the bastards knew we were coming!' Viktor Teufel exclaimed, his dark eyes full of fear and anger. He pressed his back against the hot stone of the wall, as if he feared a sniper's bullet. 'An empty barricade and the roofs full of Polish gunmen — a carefully planned trap!'

'Impossible,' Bogdan snapped irritably, trying to control his rage that his new attack had bogged down before it had really started. 'A matter of luck.'

'Then how do you explain,' Teufel began, but Bogdan silenced him with an angry movement of his big hand.

'There is no time for analysis of what went wrong. I'll leave that to generals who want a convenient excuse to sit on their fat important generals' arses and do nothing. No,' he said, his voice rising, as he made his decision, 'we must move. Act now — talk later!' He swung round to his hideous faced Chief of Staff. 'Boris!'

'General!'

'Get a Squadron dismounted and move them into the houses at the right at once.'

'And then, sir?'

'Order them to work their way onto the roof, boots off Cossack fashion, and knives.'

Boris's eyes gleamed wickedly. 'You're going to spring a trap on the Poles, General?'

Bogdan nodded, but there was no warmth in his blue eyes. 'Yes, two can play that game. All right, Boris, get them moving at once. I want them on that roof and in position to get at the Poles in ten minutes.'

Boris hurried away on his small, bandy legs, whistling happily to himself through his fleshless lips, the work of a German plastic surgeon.

Bogdan turned to Peter. 'Peter, it's going to be dangerous, but I want you with me. When we break through the Polish line, I need someone with me who can speak Fritz. I don't want those people at the Bruehl Palace firing on my Cossacks by mistake. Those Poles on the roof are bad enough.'

'Of course, General,' Peter von Kranz answered immediately. He flashed a quick look at Viktor Teufel, but the Obersturmbannführer had turned away and was apparently studying the front through his glasses with all-consuming interest. Peter shrugged. He knew that Teufel had little stomach for combat. He turned to Bogdan again. 'What's the plan, General?' he asked quickly.

'There is none, Peter,' Bogdan answered. 'The lead squadron will draw their fire and then it's up to the men of "A" to sort the Poles out.' He drew his finger across his throat to signify how they would complete that task.

'And who is to be in charge of the guinea pigs?' Peter asked, knowing the answer.

Momentarily, Bogdan touched the little sack of Don earth around his neck. Then he grinned. 'Can't you guess?'

'Here they come!' Wanda commanded shrilly. '*Pigeons, they're coming again!*'

Down below, the Cossacks were coming at the gallop. Their sabres gleaming in the copper-light, they screamed and swung them in fatalistic fury. The street echoed and re-echoed with the clatter of their horses' hooves. Foam-flecked, their hooves striking up showers of blue sparks, the horses thundered towards the barricade.

'God forgive me!' Wanda cried, and pressed her trigger.

At full gallop, a Cossack sergeant flew out of his saddle, slapped the cobbles, bounced high and lay still, his back broken. That single shot was the signal for the rest of her pigeons. Furiously they began to fire at the tightly-packed, cursing, sweating men below.

A slug slammed into the wall a metre from Bogdan. Plaster and brick showered his crimson face. He shook his head angrily and ducked low over his horse's outstretched mane. The barricade was only a matter of metres away now and he knew he must not hesitate. He must take it at the gallop or he'd be done for.

Beside him, Peter's horse whinnied piteously. Next instant it had gone down on its forelegs, flinging Peter to the cobbles. Just in time the one-armed German prevented himself from falling. Men and horses were going down all around him, but he did not hesitate. Pistol still clutched in his hand, he pelted towards the barricade for dear life, his nostrils full of hot stench of horse and the sweet smell of freshly spilled blood.

The barricade loomed up in front of Bogdan. Slugs were hitting the ground on all sides of him. He jerked at the bit and dug his spurs into the stallion's sweating flanks. *Don* sailed high into the air. Up and over. He could feel the furniture scrape the horse's belly. The stallion whinnied with pain, but he kept it on course. With a great crash it hit the cobbles on the other side. Two tons of man and mount hit the ground with an impact of 100 kmph. The stallion went down on its hindlegs. Savagely Bogdan tugged at the bit, till he rose up. A Pole sprang out of a house, machine pistol at the ready. Bogdan's sabre hissed through the air. The Pole screamed once, dropping his weapon as he fell to the cobbles, his severed head rolling into the gutter.

Bogdan breathed out hard. He was through and uninjured. But behind him his squadron was being cut to ribbons by the

Polish snipers' unerringly accurate fire. His chest heaving crazily, he stared up at the roof, shrouded in the brown smoke of small arms fire. *Where the hell was Boris?*

Wanda felt the hand touch her shoulder almost gently. She swung her head up from the butt of her sniper's rifle and recoiled with horror. A bandy-legged, little Cossack was grinning down at her, his hideously scarred face, lobster-pink. She saw the knife in his hand and flinging back her head, screamed.

It was the movement that Boris had waited for. The razor-sharp Cossack knife hissed across her upraised soft throat. Wanda screamed once. A thin red line appeared suddenly on the white skin, and grew thicker and darker by the second. Boris raised his blood-stained knife, laughing crazily and plunged it deep into her breast. Wanda's spine arched tightly like a taut bow revealing the shape of her breasts. 'Holy sow!' Boris cried in open-mouthed wonder as she died at his feet, '*a woman!*' Then he pulled himself together and withdrawing the knife with a soft sucking sound, he let her fall back onto the roof, while all around him the barefoot Cossacks slaughtered Wanda Chochim's pigeons.

It was all over in a matter of five minutes, and the laughing, triumphant Cossacks were tossing the dying snipers over the edge of the building, watching them bounce like rubber balls, as they hit the cobbles, breaking every bone and twitching convulsively in their death throes. Then they, too, lay still among the massacred Cossacks, arms flung out under the burning sky of Warsaw.

One hour later, the Black Cossacks had fought their way to within hailing distance of the Bruehl Palace, whose ornate

Baroque walls after two weeks of fighting were pocked with bullet marks like a skin disease.

Peter von Kranz pushed aside the dead Pole, behind the heap of pavestones, a neat red bullet hole bored through the centre of his youthful forehead, and cupped his hand to his mouth. 'Comrades,' he bellowed, 'this is the Black Cossack Division! Do not fire! We are coming in to relieve you! *Do not fire!*'

Finally the besieged men understood. On the roof a grey-clad figure waved his hands in recognition and placed his outstretched fingers on the top of his helmet — the infantry signal for 'rally on me' — before he ducked quickly behind the balustrade as angry Polish fire descended upon him.

Peter dropped next to Bogdan again. 'It's all right, General, they've understood.'

Bogdan nodded and peered carefully over the top of the hole. His Cossacks were crouched everywhere in the Piludski Square, weapons at alert, ready to go. It was now or never. Throwing aside all caution, he thrust his forefinger and thumb in his mouth and whistled in the Cossack fashion — once, twice, thrice.

The Black Cossacks understood. With a great throaty 'hurrah', they rose to their feet as one. In a series of crazy zig-zags they doubled across the battle littered square, men falling all the time, as the Poles opened up desperately, knowing instinctively that this was the last push. 'Come on!' Bogdan cried wildly, raising his sabre, 'do you dogs want to live for ever?'

Without another word, he launched himself over the top of the hole. His men followed, infected by his wild enthusiasm. Together they pelted towards a shattered, burnt out tram plastered with the death's head poster of the insurgents and the order '*Każdy Pocisk — Jeden Niemiec*,' '*For every bullet — a German*'. A blond youth with the red and white armband of the insurgents raised his hand to throw a grenade at the advancing officers.

Peter von Kranz fired without aiming. The man crumbled to the ground. The grenade dropped from his nerveless fingers and exploded with a blinding flash. The man was raised a metre from the ground and thrown down again like a sack of wet cement. Bogdan sprang over the shattered, blackened body and slammed into the side of the tram. He could see the desolate wreck of the palace quite clearly now, with its empty windows and the bullet torn swastika hanging limply from the pole on the roof. For a brief moment he stared at the flag he had once hated so much and wondered what he was doing here in the Piludski Square fighting Poles for the Nazis. He forced the thought from his mind and waving his sabre stepped clear of the tram, to the accompaniment of slugs striking the metal side, he was running madly for the Palace.

He cut down the Pole who tried to bar his way with his sabre. Blood fountained onto the cobbles, and he slipped to his right knee. The gesture saved his life as at that moment, a burst of machine pistol fire sawed the air where his head had just been. Behind him Boris hurled a stick grenade at the Pole hiding behind one of the bullet pocked pillars. It exploded in a thick throaty crump, taking most of the pillar with it. The Pole fell to the ground, most of his face gone. Bogdan flung the Chief Of Staff a grateful look.

Boris's terrible, livid face cracked into a mockery of a grin and he cried, carried away by the wild excitement of the attack, 'Come on, General, don't tell me you want to kneel there all day saying your prayers!'

Bogdan roared a gross obscenity and followed. Everywhere his men were now cutting down the last of the Polish defenders. An officer tried to rally his men, hammering at retreating backs in futile sobbing fury. Peter shot him and he staggered back against the Palace wall, trailing a snake of blood after him as he slipped helplessly down.

Suddenly the heart went out of the few surviving Poles, who began to throw away their weapons and raise their hands in surrender. Uncontrolled in the heady excitement of their wild charge, the Cossacks started to massacre them until Boris, hammering at them with the butt of his smoking pistol, managed to stop them lest the rest decided to go on fighting. Swiftly the firing ceased becoming a series of individual shots as the Cossacks winkled out the last of the diehard pigeons, the élite of the Polish forces, who fought to the end.

Minutes later General Bogdan strode imperiously across the debris littered floor of the old Bruehl Palace, which had once been the home of Polish royalty, towards Marshal Rainer Stahel, an ascetic-looking officer, who was waiting for him, a tired smile on his unshaven, thin face.

After Bogdan had reported, he turned to von Kranz and said: 'Tell your General, *Oberstleutnant*, that he has my warmest congratulations. Thanks to his effort this afternoon, we can really begin the final reckoning with those damned Poles.'

Yet when Peter translated Stahel's warm words of congratulation, Bogdan felt no pride, only a sense of oppressive loss for the men who had been massacred so needlessly at the barricade — and the uneasy knowledge that somehow everything was not right at his HQ.

CHAPTER 3

But Bor was not beaten yet. That night when Bogdan had linked up earlier with Marshal Stahel, General Bor stood on the roof of the house which lay above his HQ and watched the preparations for the long awaited RAF arms drop.

Below, the fifteen women of the Polish Socialist Party Militia, who had been specially chosen for the task, moved into position silently in their rubber soled shoes. Carefully like grey shadows, they arranged themselves in the cover of the tall, old houses, away from the Fritzes' preying eyes, and at the command of the heavy-bosomed, cropped-haired Sergeant, lay down on the hot cobbles.

Now there was no sound, save that of the faint wind and the odd crack of a rifle or pistol a long way off. After the victory of that afternoon, the Germans had taken off their pressure. Probably celebrating their victory in their usual swinish way, Bor guessed, by swilling down schnaps and beer, drinking themselves into insensibility. His aides searched the velvet, moonless sky with night glasses. 'Sir,' one of the aides whispered urgently, 'I think I can hear them!'

Immediately General Bor forgot the Fritzes. 'Where?' he snapped.

'Over there to the west.'

Bor cocked his head to one side, hardly daring to breathe. He knew it was vital for the continuation of the battle that his men should receive ammunition, especially the British Piat antitank weapon; soon the Fritzes would start blasting them out of their holes and sewers with heavy tank guns. Then he heard it — a faint steady droning, which grew louder by the second. 'Tell the women to get ready,' he ordered softly.

The aide doubled to the edge of the flat roof and flashed his torch once. A quick flash of blue light from below indicated that the Sergeant had heard the drone of the RAF supply planes too, and was ready for them.

But the insurgents were obviously not the only ones who had spotted the planes coming in from the west. Abruptly the Fritz searchlights began to click on everywhere. White fingers of glaring light started to part the sky, looking for the enemy. Here and there a nervous flak crew opened fire blindly into the dark sky.

Suddenly the first squadron came into view, pinpointed like silver moths in the glare. The flak swung round and began to pepper the sky with brilliantly scarlet balls of explosive fire. Steadily the planes came on, seemingly contemptuous of the enemy fire.

Bor cupped his hands round his mouth. 'Tell them to light up — *now!*' he roared above the crash and thunder of the German antiaircraft fire.

The aide shouted the order from the side of the roof, the Sergeant bellowed something. Simultaneously each of the women lying on the ground lit her hurricane lamp. A three metre V sprang into life, protected from the German's eyes, but clearly visible from above, guiding the supply planes to their dropping zones.

With a great roar, the first four-engined Halifax, which had flown half across Europe to reach Warsaw, zoomed in low over the rooftops of the old town. Six parachutes burst from its blue painted belly opening at once. A great cheer rose from the women, lying motionless on the cobbles, the spent flak falling all around them like rain. Plane after plane entered the silver halo of the massed German searchlights and braved the red inferno of the bursting shells. Parachutes blossomed everywhere. A Halifax was hit, and seemed to stagger in mid-air. Bor groaned out loud and said a quick prayer for its safety. The pilot caught it in time and the Halifax released its six chutes. As they started to drift towards the dropping zone at Napoleon Square, the plane burst into flames.

Horrified the men on the roof watched it lose height with sickening inevitability, dropping lower and lower as it crossed the Vistula. The Russian lines were only a few kilometres away. Perhaps the stricken RAF plane might make the safety of the Allied lines? But with a sudden blinding sheet of flame and a great explosion, which rocked the roof beneath the watchers' feet, the Halifax smashed into the ground on the other side of the river. In an abrupt, echoing silence, the last of the precious arms containers began to drift down to the hands waiting for them so eagerly.

But Bor knew that he needed more than arms and ammunition to defend the old city against the Germans, whom he knew from his intelligence sources behind the Fritz front, were massing for an all-out attack on his positions. Pressure had to be put on the Russians to make them resume their offensive towards the Vistula, lest German troops from the frontline were withdrawn to join the assault on his defenders. Stalin must resume the fight, if the Secret Army were to maintain its control over Warsaw!

That same night, he radioed London, thanking it for the delivery of the vital supplies and adding: 'I have decided to defend Warsaw to the limits of possibility. We possess food to last until September 7th. Ammunition is difficult — how long it will last depends on the intensity of the struggle. The possibility of holding out does not depend solely on our own powers of endurance but on material help from you, or on speedy success in Soviet operations in our sector.'

The message was handed to the British Prime Minister Winston Churchill next morning. Together with the War Cabinet he drafted a strong message to the Soviet dictator Stalin, reading: 'Whatever the rights and wrongs of the beginnings of the Warsaw rising, the people of Warsaw themselves cannot be held responsible for the decision taken. Our people cannot understand why no material help has been sent from outside… The fact that such help could not be sent on account of your Government's refusal to allow United States aircraft to land on aerodromes in Russian hands is now becoming publicly known. If the Poles in Warsaw should now be overwhelmed by the Germans, as we are told they must be within two or three days, the shock to public opinion here will be incalculable.

Out of regard for Marshal Stalin and the Soviet peoples with whom it is our earnest desire to work in future years, the War Cabinet have asked me to make this further appeal to the Soviet Government to give whatever help may be in their power, and above all to provide facilities for United States aircraft to land on your airfields for this purpose.'

Stalin replied that he was not prepared to help 'the group of criminals who have embarked on the Warsaw adventure in order to seize power, exploiting the good faith of the inhabitants of Warsaw, throwing many almost unarmed people against the German guns, tanks and aircraft.' But Churchill was not prepared to let the Warsaw Poles perish so easily; he had his own reasons for wanting to help the obscure General in far-off Warsaw. He knew now it wouldn't be long before the Germans were beaten; Hitler's 1,000 Year Empire was falling apart rapidly. The new enemy, as he saw it, would be the Russians. Stalin was not benign pipe smoking 'Uncle Joe' that Roosevelt made him out to be; he was a fanatical dictator. whose hands were red with the blood of countless Russians and foreigners. Now, he knew, it was vitally important that strong anti-Russian forces, such as Bor's Poles, should be in charge of Central Europe when the Red Army marched westwards from its own borders. As he told his cabinet colleagues in secret, he had not fought one dictator for five years to see him replaced by another one; red was just as bad as brown. The same day as he received Stalin's refusal to aid the besieged Poles, he appealed to Roosevelt in Washington to authorise the United States Army Air Corps to drop arms over Warsaw. If necessary, he urged the crippled American President, the US Flying Fortresses should land on Soviet airfields after dropping their loads, without Russian consent.

But Roosevelt, still believing he could work with the Russian dictator and not wishing to risk the shaky alliance with 'Uncle Joe' for the sake of a handful of right-wing Poles, cabled back: 'I am informed by my Office of Military Intelligence that the fighting Poles have departed from Warsaw and that the Germans are now in full control. The problem of relief for the Poles has therefore unfortunately been solved by the delay and by German action; there now appears to be nothing we can do to assist them.'

When Churchill had read the message, he let it flutter to the paper littered floor of his study and muttered through clenched teeth: 'What perfidy ... what cruel cynicism!'

And in far-away Moscow, the pock-marked, swarthy Soviet dictator puffed his hooked pipe contentedly and waited. Soon the ripe plum of Warsaw would fall into his lap of its own accord; he would not even need to shake the tree...

CHAPTER 4

Standing in the shadows outside the glare of the lamps in the operating theatre, Bogdan watched curiously as Roswitha went to work on the emaciated, naked corpse on the table. He knew she was exhausted; she had been operating all day. But she wanted to know why the Pole on the table had died. He had been delivered into their hands that morning, as a prisoner. There had not been a scratch on his body. Yet within thirty minutes he was dead. He had simply closed his eyes during interrogation by the Black Cossacks' intelligence officer and fallen dead to the floor.

Now she ran her professional eye over the painfully thin, blue-skinned corpse of the young Pole, then nodded to the masked nurse to hand her the scalpel. With a swift, expert movement, she began to make a modified Y incision, cutting from each clavicle inward towards the sternum and then straight down the torso to the pubis.

Bogdan watched with horrified fascination, as the dead man's body was carved up in sections as easily as the Cossack butcher in his native village had once sliced up a side of beef. Roswitha began to snap through the severed bones and cartilage, dictating tonelessly to the medical secretary taking notes at her side: 'Thoracic cavity … complete absence of subcutaneous fat.' She reached into the cavity and excised the heart, gasping as she said: 'heart shrunk to the size of a … a baby's fist.'

Her autopsy continued, her voice unemotional and professional as she dictated her findings: 'Duodenum … complete absence of subcutaneous fat … peritoneal cavity …

small amount of fluid, complete absence of subcutaneous fat...' At last she straightened up wearily and pulled off her mask.

'Well, doctor,' the under-surgeon, a tubby bespectacled Pole, asked, 'what's your verdict? Personally, I can't see any pathological reason why this man should have died.'

Roswitha blinked back sudden tears. 'I can tell you why he died, my dear colleague. The man's heart has shrunk to the size of a child's. There's not a gram of fat on him. You want to know why he died? It's simple. *He starved to death!*'

Silently, Bogdan waited until she had taken off her jacket. She looked pale and very worn. There were dark blue circles under her eyes and her body no longer seemed so lushly generous as it had been when he had first taken her to bed. 'Exhausted?' he said finally, leading her to the dinner table.

She nodded. 'Completely,' she answered in a husky voice. She ate slowly, carefully even, and drank little, hardly speaking, while his white-coated Cossack batman served the simple evening meal: German pea soup with sausage, and chicken cooked in the Circassian Cossack fashion, the flesh beaten to a pulp and cooked in walnut oil. Several times he pressed vodka on her. 'Take a little water for your soul's sake, Roswitha. It will put fire into your blood again.'

But she refused each time, smiling a little, though her eyes did not light up, as if she were turning some burdensome problem over in her mind. In the end he relapsed into silence too, and after the batman had cleared away the meal, he slumped in the chair opposite her, regarding her pale beautiful face in the flickering light of the candle, smoking his long Russian cigarette in moody contemplation.

Finally she broke the heavy silence herself. 'Alexei,' she said suddenly, 'why do you serve them?'

He looked across at her. 'Who? Serve who?'

She flung a quick glance at the door to see if anyone were listening. He knew the gesture well; half of Europe had been making it for years now, scared as they were of the NKVD or Gestapo. 'The Germans, why do you serve them? You are Russian after all.'

'A Cossack,' he corrected her.

'All right, a Cossack,' she said, a little impatiently. 'But they are your enemies really, aren't they?'

'*Enemies?*'

'Of course, do you really think they are concerned about the fate of you Cossacks?'

'What about the Wehrmacht generals who helped us,' he objected, 'or Peter von Kranz?'

She shrugged and her beautiful breasts moved under the thin white silk of her low-cut blouse. 'Perhaps some of them are genuinely concerned. But most of them, especially the SS, are using you. In their eyes there is nothing to distinguish you from Dirlewanger or Kaminsky.'

Bogdan was genuinely shocked. 'Roswitha, you can't mean that, my little pigeon! Dirlewanger and Kaminsky are bandits whose only loyalty is to loot. But we Cossacks have a cause. We fight for them because they will enable us to return to our homeland,' he said the words longingly, 'our Quiet Don. You must understand that!'

She did not speak and slowly Bogdan rose to his feet and stared at his own image in the long, flyblown mirror, as if to reassure himself that the lean, hard-faced man staring back at him was the same person he had just been talking about. Behind him he could see her watching him with a new, intent light in her tired eyes. Suddenly he swung round and looked down at her. 'Roswitha,' he demanded, the gentleness gone from his voice now, 'what are you getting at?'

The Polish surgeon took her time answering, blue smoke rings rising from the long cigarette held between her nicotine-stained fingers, as if she were finding it difficult to formulate her words. 'Alexei — little Alexei,' she said finally. 'Sit down, I've got something important to tell you.'

Obediently he did as she asked, and waited.

'I respect you, Alexei — as a man,' she began a little hesitantly. 'But I don't respect the cause you serve. The Fritzes came here to Poland as conquerors in thirty-nine. For five years they have been here, and do you see any signs of freedom for us Poles?' Her voice was hard now, even harsh. 'And in your own homeland, was it any different? They were there too for three years and what did they do? Oh yes, they gave some of the minorities their independence. But why? Because it was the easiest way to control the Russian people — divide and conquer. Even if they won the war — which they won't now — they would never give you Cossacks or us Poles our freedom. A post-war world in which the Germans were the victors would be a cruel all-German empire, ruled with an iron hand from Berlin. There would be no freedom for the subject peoples.'

She leaned forward eagerly and Bogdan, sombre and silent, was conscious of her body. 'Alexei, the Fritzes are lying to you. They're using you. When they've finished with you, they'll toss you to one side, or put you back in prison again if you open your mouth to protest. Alexei Bogdan,' her voice rose, all caution thrown to the winds now, 'learn this before it is too late, *and act*. You and your Cossacks are expendable!'

Bogdan did not reply. He was too shocked. He knew now where the leak was in his HQ and how the Polish snipers had known of the Cossack attack towards the Bruehl Palace. *His mistress was their spy!*

It was a conclusion that Obersturmbannführer Viktor Teufel had reached, too. As August gave way to September, 1944, he decided that the Polish doctor had been using her position as Bogdan's mistress to pass on information to the AK; and it had not taken him long to discover how she was doing it.

Her method was simple and gruesome. Every evening after she had finished operating for the day, the men who had died on the operating table were deposited outside the back of the big hospital, often piled up six deep like logs of wood, and covered from prying eyes by bloodstained tarpaulins. As soon as it was dark, a grumpy, moustached Pole appeared with his cart, pulled by a weary, ancient nag to take them away to the mass graves in the park, outside the hospital boundaries. The Cossacks were a superstitious bunch and General Bogdan had ordered that no body should remain overnight near his HQ, in case his men started seeing ghosts, common enough with the Cossack backward boys.

But as Teufel had seen with his own eyes, when the old Pole was finished with his gruesome task of covering the ghastly shattered bodies of the dead with lime and earth, he did not return to his bunk next to the hospital's boiler room. Instead, using the special pass he possessed, permitting him to be out after curfew, he disappeared in the direction of the enemy lines where he met one of the teenage *Kanalarki* to whom he passed on whatever information he possessed. *That special pass had been signed by Frau Doktor Graefin Roswitha Jankowski!*

'I don't believe it!' Peter von Kranz exclaimed when Teufel told of his discovery one early September afternoon. 'Bogdan couldn't be that stupid!'

Teufel grinned unpleasantly. 'You don't know your Cossacks, Peter,' he sneered. 'They can't see further than the end of their tails when it comes to a piece of skirt. A woman like Countess Jankowski can twist a Cossack cowboy like Bogdan around her little finger any time she likes.'

'Proof?' Peter snapped coldly. He knew just how much Teufel hated the Cossack General; he would do anything in his power to humiliate him as long as it didn't affect his own position.

Swiftly, enjoying the detail he was able to offer, Teufel described what he had discovered about the Polish woman, while Peter listened stony-faced. Finally Peter said: 'And what do you propose to do, Viktor?'

Teufel's dark face broke into a cold smile, 'Arrest her at the earliest possible occasion, of course.'

'Have you got all your cups in your cupboard, man!' Peter exploded. 'I haven't the slightest idea what Bogdan's real feelings are for the Countess. She might be just something he needs in bed, as far as I know. But I *do* know this. If you arrest her now, we — the German command — are in for trouble.'

'What do you mean? The Polish bitch is a spy, isn't she? She must be eradicated at once.'

Peter shook his blond head in mock dismay. 'Don't you realise what Bogdan's reaction would be if we did that now? His whole allegiance to our cause is in the balance. He hates fighting the Poles; after all he joined our cause to fight against communism, not them. We must keep him sweet until we have dealt with the insurgents, then we can tackle the Countess.'

'So what do you do?' Viktor asked. 'We can't let the woman go on revealing our plans to those damned Poles?'

Peter stroked his nose thoughtfully. 'You're right, of course, Viktor,' he answered after a moment. 'I must dream up some sort of scheme to tighten up the General's personal security... Leave it to me, I'll think of something to prevent him talking to her about his plans.' He smiled a little wanly. 'But it's damnably difficult to come between a man and his mistress.'

'*Mattress*, you mean,' Viktor snapped scornfully, not returning his smile. 'And the woman?'

'Let us leave her in place until we have finished off the insurgents.'

'All right, all right, I'll accept your solution,' Viktor said slowly. 'But I have one request, Peter. When the time comes to arrest Roswitha Jankowski, I want to reserve that particular little task for myself.' His hand fell to his pistol and Peter von Kranz knew that his next words would seal the beautiful Countess's fate. Obersturmbann-führer Teufel would have no mercy on her. She would receive the same old treatment: a swift car ride into the country after dark, a bullet blasted into the back of the head and the cause of death given as 'shot while trying to escape'.

Slowly he nodded his head and said in a weary voice, 'Yes, Viktor, she'll be all yours, once we have taken Warsaw...'

CHAPTER 5

The Battle for Warsaw continued in all its bloody fury. As the first week of September, 1944, gave way to the second, and Warsaw had still not surrendered, Reichsführer Himmler called Bach-Zelewski to his HQ. His usual pale face was flushed with anger and his eyes sparkled with unaccustomed animation. He hardly gave the big East Prussian the chance to enter the door of his office before he launched into a full scale attack on his method of conducting the battle. The words bubbled from his mouth in a seemingly endless flow, specks of foam caught at the edges of his mouth. 'In three devils' name, Bach-Zelewski what are you up to in Warsaw? You don't think you'll earn the piece of tin the Führer promised you like this? I ordered you to raze the city, wipe out every damn Pole! Fight terror with terror. Why haven't you done it?'

Bach-Zelewski took off his glasses and wiped them nervously. 'I'm fighting all out, but our losses have been horrifying. In some of the assault units they have been up to fifty percent of the effectives —'

'I'm not interested,' Himmler interrupted him bitterly. 'Results are what count. Man, Bach-Zelewski, as an experienced soldier you should know you can't make an omelette without breaking eggs. Your men should be proud to die for Folk, Fatherland and Führer. What is Dirlewanger doing, eh? There's a man who is not afraid of a little blood, a few casualties!'

'He's resting, Reichsführer. He's already lost over two thirds of his men,' the big Commander answered unhappily, knowing what Himmler's reaction would be.

'*Resting!*' Himmler exploded. 'One of the most aggressive units you possess is resting because it has suffered a few knocks. My God, General, nations are born of blood! Blood must flow to make a nation strong. If —' he caught himself in time, before he launched into his favourite subject: the superiority of Nordic blood. 'And what of your Cossack cowboys? I suppose they are out of the line resting, too?'

Bach-Zelewski nodded, his face unhappy. 'I thought it better to pull them out after their link up with Stahel so that they could ready themselves for the final attack.'

Himmler shook his head in wonder. 'Heaven, arse and twine, General, you can't win a battle by resting! So Dirlewanger needs reinforcements? He will get them by the thousand. The prisons and penal barracks are full of crooks and criminals, only too eager to go and fight the Poles for their Fatherland' — he allowed himself a faint, cynical smile — 'if they can buy their freedom by doing so.'

He took a quick breath. 'As for your Cossack cowboys. Why the devil should I care about their casualties or whether they are rested or not? Throw them into the battle at once. The more dead Cossacks and Poles there are, the fewer of the Slavic scum we will have to deal with when the final day of reckoning comes. Bach-Zelewski, time is running out. The Führer is breathing down my neck for results. We can't endure the running sore of Warsaw much longer. It won't be long before the Ivans attack again on the Vistula and then we'll need every man we've got.' He licked the spittle from the corners of his thin, cruel lips. 'I'll give you another week, General. By the end of it, I want you to report to me here that the Battle of Warsaw is over — that the capital is razed to the ground. Clear?'

'Clear, Reichsführer!'

'Heil Hitler!' Himmler swept out of the office, leaving a downcast Bach-Zelewski staring miserably at the Führer's portrait on the wall.

CHAPTER 6

The sound was unlike anything the hard-pressed defenders of the Polish capital had heard before in the five-week long battle. As the blood-red ball of the sun appeared over the ruined roofs, a dull groaning noise was heard in the distance. In the debris littered streets, the water carriers halted and listened; the women stripping the flesh off the night's fresh crop of dead horses paused in their gruesome task, knives glinting blood-red in the rising sun, and turned their weary heads in the direction of the sound; in their underground HQs, the staff officers, faces pale and strained, waited poised in front of the situation maps, knowing instinctively that the Fritzes had thought up a yet more terrible means of death and destruction for them.

Twice that strange uncanny new noise sounded. Far, far away to the west, there were faint pink flashes. Nothing happened; for what seemed a very long time, nothing happened. The staff officers underground had already counted up to ten, when the morning stillness was shattered by a baleful, enraged scream, elemental in its fury, but manmade for all that. The water carriers dropped their pails and ran for cover. The women hurled themselves to the cobbles next to the bloody horse carcasses, hands pressed over their heads.

With an appalling crash the first great 1,500 lb concrete shell, fired from 8,000 metres away by the Karl Morser, slapped into the Old City. The effect was appalling. Dismembered bodies flew everywhere, splashing the new ruins with blood. Men and women lay writhing in their final agonies in street after street. The gutters ran with a red torrent of blood. Whole blocks came tumbling down as if made of card. Almost at once the next shell came crashing down, the signal for the whole weight of Bach-Zelewski's artillery to begin its softening up process. Simultaneously, twenty 75mm assault guns, six 150mm guns, four 280mm howitzers, six multiple rocket launchers, eighteen aerial mine throwers and a battalion of Tiger tanks, armed with 88mm cannon roared into action.

Under the impact of this terrible avalanche of fire, the medieval houses of the Old City came down by their scores, burying hundreds of men and women beneath their burning ruins. In their holes and sewers, the men of the Secret Army huddled together, cowering in misery, their hands pressed over their ears, as the earth shuddered and shook with inhuman violence. The air was rent with the shriek and roar of the bombs, the thick heavy crash of the howitzer shells, the whine of the armour piercing slugs — a sustained nightmarish howl. And then, as abruptly as it had started, the barrage stopped. Slowly, very slowly, the defenders raised their heads above the edge of their holes like incredibly old men. Awed, white-eyed with shock, coughing in the acrid yellow smoke of the explosives, they stared unbelievingly at the new shape of their city which was beginning to emerge from the fog of war.

But not for long. For now they could hear the rattle of tank tracks coming ever louder down the streets which led into the Old City and the hoarse triumphant cries in German. Dirlewanger's SS men were moving in to the attack.

'*Stand to ... stand to,*' the frantic cries went up on all sides. Whistles blew shrilly. Officers pulled themselves together and bellowed orders. Men picked up their weapons with numb fingers. Dirlewanger's murderers were coming...

The Dirlewanger men poured a hail of phosphorus grenades into the hospital. As it started to burn white-robed medics screamed to the wounded to get up and run for it. Flames raced through the body littered hallways. Burning, screaming men threw themselves out of the upper storey windows, hitting the cobbles like bags of wet cement. The hospital walls turned a cherry-red with the heat. Still the Dirlewanger's fired grenade after grenade at the building, screaming with hysterical laughter every time some flaming wretch flung himself out of the window. Finally the walls bulged outwards, and great sections of brickwork gave way and fell hissing to the street scattering flame. Below, patients with wildly burning paper bandages, danced like dervishes. When the Dirlewanger's went in to loot the gutted shell, they found the stairs clogged by charred corpses, reduced to the size of pygmies by the terrific heat.

That afternoon the Dirlewanger's finally took the Old Arsenal after a morning of murderous combat. As usual they had no time to take prisoners. Finding a hose pipe, they started to spray the cellars, which were full of wounded, with gasoline.

In vain the Poles pleaded for mercy in broken German. The Dirlewanger's were deaf to their pleas. A *Scharführer*, his one eye covered with a black patch, tossed a match into the gas-soaked bodies and leapt back roaring with laughter.

The first cellar exploded in a sheet of orange flame, which turned the wounded Poles into writhing human torches. Some had strength enough to crawl to the barred windows, where with blazing hands they wrenched desperately at the bars. The Dirlewanger's battered at the rapidly blackening claws with their rifle butts, enjoying the sport.

One Pole managed to escape from the inferno, and doused a bucket of water over his burning body. Crawling on all fours in a hissing cloud of steam, he crept up the stairs, trailing his charred flesh in long strips behind him. As he sucked in great gulps of fresh air, he became aware of the one-eyed *Scharführer*, whose heavy boots, drowned by the screams of burning men, had followed his painful progress. The German placed his pistol at the base of the Pole's skull and pressed the trigger. It shattered like a china cup.

Burning, looting, raping, slaughtering, the homosexual SS Colonel's bunch of criminals advanced deeper and deeper into the Old City. Place after place fell before their drunken fury. The Police Command HQ … the Ministry of Home Affairs … the Central Telephone Exchange… Nothing was able to stand up against their attack. The Dirlewanger's killed indiscriminately — German, Pole, Russian, Ukrainian, man, woman or child. Anyone not belonging to their own murderous mob was eliminated without a moment's hesitation.

That evening Colonel Grez, Bach-Zelewski's Chief of Staff, drove up to Dirlewanger's HQ to protest about the conduct of his troops. He found the SS Colonel toying with his delicate, handsome 'adjutant', playfully fastening looted pearl earrings in his ears and ruffling his blond hair delightedly. 'Dirlewanger,' he roared red-faced, while the other man ignored his presence, 'I must protest in the strongest terms at the behaviour of your men this afternoon!' Beside himself with fury, he cried, 'My God, man, do you know that when they took the Marie-Curie Radium Institute, they shot the doctors and nurses out of hand, and they even raped women suffering from terminal cancer! How can you tolerate that kind of conduct —'

The rest of the sentence suddenly froze on the Chief of Staff's lips. Dirlewanger's bodyguard had levelled their machine pistols directly at him.

'But you can't do this to me!' he stuttered. 'I'm General Bach-Zelewski's official representative!'

'Of course I can,' Dirlewanger laughed. 'Dirlewanger can do anything!' He nodded swiftly to his bodyguard.

Two of the hulking thugs pressed their machine pistols into the fat Colonel's stomach, breathing stale vodka over him. 'Move,' they commanded throatily.

The Colonel moved. As they thrust him out of the door into the burning darkness, he glimpsed Dirlewanger pressing his mouth against the pretty boy's. He shuddered with disgust and went back to his car.

That same night the Poles counter-attacked. They caught the Dirlewanger's in the newly captured Telephone Exchange off guard. They were all drunk, even the sentries, enjoying themselves with the women they had dragged screaming off the streets.

The Polish assault party showed no mercy. The Dirlewanger's and the unlucky women were shot where they lay or copulated like so many animals on the floor. Swiftly the Poles took floor after floor, carried forward — in spite of their losses — by a great overwhelming anger. Finally only a handful of survivors held out on the roof.

At midnight they offered to surrender. 'We'll come down with our hands up,' a Polish-speaking Dirlewanger offered fearfully, sobered up now by what had happened to his comrades in the last terrible thirty minutes.

'No, don't come down,' the hard-eyed Polish Commandant ordered. 'Just drop your weapons and remain where you are. We'll come up.'

Moments later the Dirlewanger's were all disarmed and the young Poles were eagerly gathering up their discarded weapons, while their Commandant eyed the men who had committed such terrible crimes that day. Suddenly he snapped a harsh order in Polish.

'No,' the Polish-speaking Dirlewanger quavered. 'Spare us!' He dropped to his knees, tears streaming down his face, wringing his hands in an ecstasy of fear.

'Him, first!' the Polish Commandant ordered, his voice harsh and unyielding.

Two young men darted forward and seized the sobbing Dirlewanger soldier. With a grunt they heaved him up and hurled him over the side of the building. He hit the cobbles below trailing his long drawn-out scream of death behind him.

One by one, struggling and screaming, his comrades followed him over the side. 'Saves ammo that way,' the Commandant commented coldly, 'and we've done the world a service, lads.'

Minutes later the Polish assault party had slunk back into the stinking sewers from which it had come.

When Dirlewanger heard of the slaughter of the Telephone Exchange garrison, he took a terrible revenge. 'How many did they kill?' he demanded hoarsely from the wide-eyed Sturmbannführer, whose company had found the bodies.

'Twenty, Brigadenführer.'

'Right, I want two hundred Polack prisoners before this night is out. I don't care how you get them, but it's got to be two hundred — ten for each one of our dead. I'll teach those Polish pigs to respect the Dirlewanger Brigade!'

By dawn the Sturmbannführer had his prisoners together: a long column of civilians of both sexes. Children, cripples, pregnant women, old folks in bathchairs, some of them half-naked, shivering in the dawn cold. The Sturmbannführer had dragged them straight from their beds in the long-regained suburbs, not wanting to risk his men's lives attacking the Polish positions to find the prisoners Dirlewanger demanded.

Dirlewanger, hands on hips, booted legs apart, viewed the pathetic procession contemptuously. Then he turned to his interpreter: 'Tell them that in the old days when Nero wanted to execute his prisoners, he first tore off their genitals with special metal claws. Tell them that.' Brigadenführer Dirlewanger, once a doctor of philosophy at Frankfurt University before being deprived of his title in 1935 for molesting a minor, was proud of his classical education.

He waited till the interpreter had finished, then said.

'But we Dirlewanger's have modernised the process. We haven't the time for individual treatment, however titillating it may be.' His voice rose and he snapped out an order. 'String them up!'

The waiting troopers leapt forward to tie up their prisoners, forcing their legs apart, tossing the cripples out of their chairs and trussing them up like animals as they lay on the cold ground. Finally they were finished and the troopers backed away swiftly as the flamethrower operators advanced on their shrieking victims.

'*Now!*' Dirlewanger ordered when they were fifty metres from their victims.

The operators came to a halt.

'And aim low, as ordered!' Dirlewanger yelled, as the operators pressed their triggers.

There was a great hush. Then from fourteen flamethrowers, scarlet, oil-tinged tongues of flame shot forward and wreathed the helpless Poles' lower bodies with their scorching fury. They screamed in agony but the operators had no mercy. They pressed their triggers time and time again until their fuel was exhausted. Before their eyes the Poles' flesh bubbled like paint.

By the morning of the second day of the new offensive, Dirlewanger had lost one third of his effectives. But still he was advancing with the same speed as on the previous day, using the whole range of newly developed German devices which Himmler had rushed up to his Brigade for the attack. Goliaths, electrically fired multiple mortars, the napalm rocket, and the most terrible weapon of all — the *Taifun System*.

For some time now, Dirlewanger had realised that the Poles had the ability to move under and behind his positions by means of the maze of sewers that ran beneath the Old City. He had tried to cut them off by establishing listening posts above the manhole covers, which would open fire with grenades and flamethrowers as soon as the presence of Poles was reported. But the listening post system was too haphazard and long-winded a process for the impatient Colonel Dirlewanger. The new weapon system now offered him a swift means of removing the Polish vermin. As he confided confidently to his cronies: 'The *Taifun'll* clear the swine out of the sewers like a dose of salts going through a constipated whore!'

On the afternoon of the second day, the device was tried out for the first time, in the sewers that ran outwards from Napoleon Square. Everywhere, the specially trained engineers pumped the explosive gas down the manholes which dotted the battle littered square. Finally they were ready. 'Ignite!' the officer in charge commanded above the snap and crackle of small arms fire.

The gas was lit. The first muffled crump of an explosion beneath their feet was followed immediately by another and another. The ground trembled as the gas exploded all along the sewer system, setting off a chain reaction like an explosion of fire damp in a coal mine. Finally the explosions died away and it was time to open the main sewer lid. 'Open up!' Dirlewanger cried, and craned his head forward eagerly. The lid rattled to the cobbles. For a moment or two they could see nothing until the thick white cloud of smoke had cleared away. And then Dirlewanger saw what he had expected to see. The dead Poles, bodies crushed to jelly by the blast, were plastered to the sides of the sewers like rows of grotesque postage stamps. Dirlewanger clapped his hands in delight.

And now the Poles started to surrender by the score, throwing away their weapons in terror, clambering out of the sewers, babbling incoherently, pleading on their knees to be allowed to surrender. The scores became hundreds and hundreds became thousands. There were too many of them for even Dirlewanger's killers to slaughter. They swamped the decimated Brigade. In the end, Dirlewanger wired off empty squares and corralled his ragged, emaciated prisoners thus, ordering his men: 'Not a bite to eat for them. Not a drop of water, let the Polish pigs croak... We haven't got the ammunition to waste on them anymore.'

At first, the starving Poles contented themselves with retrieving their excrement from the gutters, and with their bare hands picking out the undigested bits of millet — their standard diet for the last four weeks — from the loathsome mess, while their captors jeered: '*Look at the Polack shit eaters!*'

But their ravenous hunger overcame them and they started to eat their own dead. In the beginning they did so furtively, stealing among the dead to hack off a limb and hurrying off to a dark corner to gnaw at the raw flesh; or smashing in a skull, the bones as thin as a child's now, and scooping out a handful of grey brain matter to swallow down in one greedy gulp.

Some of their comrades tried to stop them, forming anti-cannibal patrols, but when the leader of the anti-cannibal group found his own brother's corpse had been eaten, he went mad, howling on all fours like a mad dog. After this the resistance ceased. Now the cannibals roamed the cages in packs, swinging severed limbs like weapons, defying anyone to stop them.

And all the time Dirlewanger's terrible Brigade advanced closer and closer to the centre of the Old City. Soon it would be the turn of the Black Cossacks to launch their attack and drive the ever-weakening Poles down to the Vistula and their doom.

CHAPTER 7

The Black Cossack attack took the Poles completely by surprise. The fake plan of attack which Peter von Kranz had fed Bor by means of the frightened Polish cart driver, had led him to believe the Cossacks would attack directly into the Old City where the main body of the Secret Army was dug in.

Instead the Cossacks burst out of their positions in the Mokotow suburb and pushed rapidly forward, swinging right at the recaptured, shattered wreck of the Telephone Exchange, and heading for the Poniatowski Bridge. At their head, Bogdan flung himself into the new battle with a reckless disregard for his own safety. Slashing and hacking his way through the surprised Polish defences, lashing his sweat lathered stallion cruelly, he led the Black Cossacks' 1st Squadron as if he were a young Imperial Cavalry Lieutenant of eighteen, and not a divisional commander in his mid-forties. And as he rode, his mind was full of Roswitha's last words to him: 'We have all been betrayed, Alexei. You by the Germans — we Poles by the Allies. And in the end who will gain all?' She had shrugged, no longer caring that she had betrayed her secret to him, as if she were placing herself willingly at his mercy now. 'The Russians!' Then she had reached up and said softly, 'Kiss me for the last time, little Alexei. Now our time is running out.'

Over and over the words ran through his head that long, bloody first day of the new attack, surmounting the clatter of his horse's hooves, the chatter of the machine guns, the crash of the cannon: '*We have all been betrayed!*'

When Bor learned of the new attack towards the vital Vistula bridge, he knew the end was near. In the Old City, the AK's agony was reaching its height. Food, water and ammunitions were running out rapidly; his doctors had to operate without anaesthetics; and dysentery was rife among those defenders still on their feet. Hour by hour, his defensive perimeter was growing increasingly smaller, with his force crowded into the shattered ruins of the 300 houses, out of the thousand with which they had begun their defence of the Old City.

In a desperate attempt to save the situation, he ordered Pelczynski and his most experienced battlefield commander Colonel Ziemski to attack the Black Cossacks in the flank. Pelczynski would lead a diversionary attack on Dirlewanger's HQ in the old Royal Castle, while Ziemski would command the main attack against the Cossacks. The attack against the Cossacks had hardly got underway, when red and green German flares started to hiss into the grey morning sky everywhere to Ziemski's front. A spy had betrayed the operation to the enemy! Doggedly the Poles pressed home their attack. But the Cossacks, well dug in for a change, met them with a wall of fire. The Poles went down by the dozen. With desperate courage they came on, again and again. But in the end they broke and streamed back the way they had come, scuttling fearfully for the cover of the ruins and sewers.

That afternoon the German Stukas came screaming down from the burning sky over Warsaw — squadron after squadron of them. Every fifteen minutes a desperate Bach-Zelewski, determined to break the Polish resistance at last, flung in a new squadron. When they had done their deadly work, the Germans threw in fresh infantry. The battle swayed back and forth, with no quarter given or expected. The Radziwill Palace, a Polish stronghold, was captured and recaptured. The main

Polish Secret Army hospital, John the Pious, fell into German hands, and remained there. Gradually the steam went out of the German attack, in the face of the desperate Polish counterattacks, as that terrible day slowly came to an end. All the same, the Germans had succeeded in capturing and holding on to three important salients in the Polish defences to the north and south.

Wearily General Bor ascended to his observation post to stare at the darkening Old City for the last time. It was a burning stone desert: a vista of rubble, broken only by a solitary wall, or lone chimney, outlined starkly against the cruel red of the flames. The Church of Our Lady, the John the God Hospital, the Blessed Sacrament Convent — all those buildings which had once been the pride of pre-war Poland had gone.

For a moment he felt a wave of self-hatred well up within him for what he had done to Warsaw and its citizens; then he repressed the feeling. He had done it all for the future of Poland. 'Pelczynski,' he said, turning to the tired, dirty-faced Chief of Staff standing in silent, awed contemplation of the burning city.

'Sir?'

'We're about finished, Pelczynski,' he said, without any emotion, almost conversationally, as if remarking on the state of the weather.

'I think so, sir,' his Chief of Staff answered in the same tone.

For a long time, Bor did not speak, his thin face haggard and worn in the flames. 'I shall have to surrender, Pelczynski.'

Pelczynski nodded silently.

'I shall stay with those who are unable to get out, of course.'

'Of course, sir.'

'But I must give those who are unwounded and willing to fight on, a chance. The young have surprising powers of recovery. Do you remember how we were as young officers in '20, eh?' He laughed softly, sadly. 'Full of piss and vinegar, was how we described it.'

'We were coarser in those days, sir.'

'And younger.'

'Yes, younger.' Pelczynski stared down at the ruined mess of the Stare Miasto, as if he were trying to see himself as a proud young Captain of Cavalry riding down that same street at the head of his men, drunk with their victory over the Red Army.

Bor cleared his throat. 'We must ensure that those youngsters have a way out.'

'The river line is blocked now, sir, and the Fritzes are too firmly in control to the west and north of the Old City to allow us to get them out that way.' Already Pelczynski knew he, too, would remain behind with his beloved Commander.

'So?' Bor said tonelessly, 'there is the sewer system to the south through the Mokotow suburb.'

'But those damned Cossacks are firmly entrenched there, sir. With our strength, it would be impossible for our young people to break through their defences.'

Bor stared at him for a long moment; then he said softly: 'Who said anything about fighting the Cossacks, Pelczynski? The time has come to talk to General Alexei Bogdan.'

'But he is the enemy, sir!' his Chief of Staff protested.

'Yes, but he is a Slav as well, my dear General…'

General Bor was not the only one who realised that the end was near in Warsaw. The same day that a victorious yet somehow downcast General Bogdan galloped at the head of his triumphant Cossacks up to the eastern end of the Poniatowski Bridge, Obersturmbannführer Teufel walked confidently into Peter von Kranz's office at the Black

Cossacks' HQ, without knocking.

'Peter, I want her!' he barked without any preliminaries.

The one-armed Colonel dropped his wooden pen onto the desk. He knew immediately what Teufel meant, but he pretended not to. 'Want whom, Viktor?' he asked.

The SS officer, seized a chair, swung it round and sat down, his arms folded over its hard back. 'Don't play games with me, Peter von Kranz. The Poles have about had it. Now I want the Polish whore you promised me. She has a debt in blood to pay, as you damn well know!'

Peter sighed wearily. Outside, a fresh convoy of wounded had arrived and the morning stillness was suddenly broken by the cries of the orderlies and the moans of the wounded, being sorted out for the dressing station or the Elzbietanek Hospital. He knew Teufel was right. The Polish doctor, who would soon be operating on those men outside, deserved death. She had spied on them and betrayed their plans to the Poles; she had blood on her hands. But hadn't they all?

'You're right, Viktor,' he said wearily. 'But how will Bogdan take it when he finds out that his mistress has been arrested for spying? And by you in person!'

'I've already thought of that, Peter,' the SS officer replied. 'I have been planning the whole operation very carefully for a whole week now. She won't be arrested by me. I will appear to have nothing to do with the matter. She will be taken publicly at her work; then Countess Jankowski will disappear quietly from the face of the earth.'

'How?' Peter demanded.

Viktor Teufel grinned and answered in one word, 'Gestapo.'

Peter shuddered.

CHAPTER 8

The four Gestapo men standing at the door of the packed operating theatre looked like a caricature of all the Gestapo men she had ever seen over these last five years. They were all fat and middle-aged, their bulk covered in identical ankle-length green leather coats. All wore the same tall felt hat, its brim pulled deep over their red, bejowled faces; and all had the same empty eyes of the sadist.

The senior one thrust a metal badge at her and mumbled, without removing the stub of cheap cigar from his thick, wet, lower lip: '*Geheime Staatspolizei*! Kommissar Hackmann. You the Countess Roswitha Jankowski?'

She nodded, her eyes above the white tight mask, revealing no fear, just a great weariness.

'Good. Get that overall off and come with us!'

'But can't you see — I'm operating.' She pointed with her bloody scalpel at the still, naked body on the table, its leg twisted round at an impossible angle, the white bone splinters flecking the bloody gore of the knee.

'You heard — *komm mit, Weib*!' Hackmann grunted. Routinely and without rancour, he hit her across the face.

She staggered back against the wall, the scalpel falling from her fingers. The operating staff gasped. The little bespectacled under-surgeon muttered angrily and clenched his gloved fist. 'All right, all right,' she said hurriedly, fumbling with her mask to reveal the dull red mark of Hackmann's hand across her deathly pale face, 'I'll come with you, just let me get my coat and bag.' She indicated the room next door. Hackmann nodded to one of his subordinates in his stolid way. 'Look 'em over, Hans,' he commanded, taking his eyes off her for a moment and thus failing to see her pick up the bloody scalpel and conceal it in the long sleeve of her dress.

In the Opel, Hackmann and Hans, his pale-eyed, gold-toothed subordinate, beat her about the face in a routine sort of way as they sped through the darkening fir forests, calling her a 'Polish whore', 'a sow of a spy' and the like without any enthusiasm. For them it was routine stuff; they had made arrests like this often in the past eleven years of the 1,000 Year Reich, first Germans, then Jews and Communists; and then men and women from a dozen European nationalities. It was a job of work, which ensured them 400 Reichsmarks a month, three squares a day, and the assurance that the short, dangerous life of the frontline, would not be their lot. But the half-hearted slapping gave Roswitha courage. At first she had been prepared to submit to her fate. But now the characteristic obstinacy of her race, the pawn of both Germans and Russians for over two centuries, surged up within her. Her green eyes flashed angrily and she spat at Hackmann: 'Take your paws off me, you fat oaf!' Suddenly she reached forward and ripped her nails down the side of his fat face.

'So that is how you want to play, you Polack bitch, eh?' Hackmann cried, a new light coming into his bored eyes, as the blood began to trickle down his face. He reached out his hands. With fingers that resembled fat German sausages, he took hold of her full breasts and squeezed hard. She screamed with pain and fell back against the back of the seat, her skirt riding up to reveal her legs.

The pale-eyed Hans winked at his superior officer. 'Look at the legs on her, *Kommissar*!' He whistled softly through his gold-teeth. 'Go all the way to her arse, I'll be bound!' He took one and squeezed it gently, then ran his hand up under her skirt until he found what his greedy fingers sought.

'Stop that, Hans, *at once*!' Hackmann barked, taking in the woman's exposed body in all its splendour.

Reluctantly the Gestapo man released his hold. Hastily she pulled down her skirt, as he grumbled, 'But it's a pity to waste all that talent, *Kommissar*? I mean —' He didn't complete his sentence, but indicated the dark glade ahead where they had pre-arranged that she should be 'shot while attempting to escape', as the Obersturmbann-führer had ordered. Kommissar Hackmann licked his lips, which were suddenly dry. 'I think, Hans,' he said in a voice that was not quite under control, 'I shall have to take the bitch to headquarters after all and ask her a few questions first.'

Hans winked one eye solemnly; he knew what the Kommissar had in mind.

He forced her first to drink vodka, pulling her head back by her long blonde hair, pouring it down her throat directly from the bottle. She let him. In her present mood it would have no effect upon her, but the crimson-faced puffing Kommissar did not know that: his attention was concentrated solely on what she had between her legs.

He took a couple of drinks himself, grinning at her with his fat, sweat lathered face in the red light the table lamp cast on the sofa. 'To get in the right mood, you know?... You as a doctor'll know, that yer pistol doesn't fire as quickly when you get to my age?'

She said nothing; she waited.

He dropped the empty bottle to the floor. His big hand clutched at the front of her dress. 'They tell me you doctors know tricks in bed that are ten times more exciting than anything we common folk can do,' he gasped. 'Is that true, come on ... *tell me*!'

'*Yes,*' she whispered huskily, faking passion.

'What will you do?'

'Anything you want,' she answered, allowing him to force her legs apart, feeling his weight descend upon her.

'*This*!' he breathed harshly.

'*Good ... good,*' she breathed in feigned ecstasy, head thrust back over the edge of the sofa, fingers fumbling desperately for the scalpel hidden in her sleeve.

'You'll get the lot!' he cried.

She found the scalpel. She steadied herself, taking a firmer grip of it. Carefully, with her free hand, she searched his fat back, as if he were a patient, looking for the exact spot where she would make the incision, above the heart.

'*Liebling ... Liebling,*' he was murmering.

She plunged the scalpel deep into his heart. His spine arched and his eyes were suddenly wide-open and staring, as he slumped over her in death.

Now she was in complete control of herself, knowing instinctively what she had to do next. Swiftly crossing the room on her bare feet, she pulled his pistol out of the holster, snapped off the safety-catch and wrapped the pistol in a cushion. Carefully she deposited the hidden pistol on the sofa.

She pulled off the rest of her ruined dress. Naked, with her white body gleaming with the sheen of sweat, she went to the door and half-opened it. The pale-faced Hans was still there, listening, his loins hidden by an old copy of the *Völkischer Beobachter.*

He looked at her knowingly, half-coyly, his pale eyes taking in her nakedness offered now so freely to his gaze, her hair hanging carelessly over the side of her flushed, hectic face, and made the wrong guess: the one she wanted him to make. 'You can come in now,' she said. 'He said it was all right.' She opened the door a little wider and revealed the Kommissar's fat, naked body slumped on the sofa, his back to the plush, mouth wide-open as if he were fast asleep.

'You mean?' He made a universal obscene gesture, his mouth slack and a little unbelieving.

She shrugged carelessly, hiding her eyes from him, like a woman completely broken and indifferent. 'What is it to me?'

'It might be nothing for you, missus, but I can do with a jump. I haven't had a bit for weeks now.' Hastily he ripped off his boots, sniggering that a 'gentleman doesn't go to bed with his shoes on'.

It was then as he bent down over the second jackboot, that she placed the pistol against the back of his flat skull and blew him to eternity, the explosion muffled by the cushion. Grabbing the shattered body, before it hit the floor, she lowered it noiselessly and began stripping it with fingers that were surprisingly deft. She felt completely detached and even had time to notice that the Gestapo man was circumcised — unusual for a German — and that someone had bungled his appendix operation rather badly.

Minutes later she was dressed in his suit, her hair tucked in well beneath the big felt hat, staring at herself in Hackmann's mirror which he had insisted — with a leer — on placing at the end of the couch, so that he could 'get the full effect'. She looked a little unconvincing, yet in the half-light she felt she'd pass as a man.

Quickly she thrust Hackmann's pistol in the pocket of the ill-fitting tweed suit, put on the leather coat and ripped open the lining of a pocket so that she could grab the pistol quickly if she needed it.

But the two bored sentries, lounging in the red and white striped sentry boxes outside the Gestapo HQ didn't even look up as she passed with a subdued, '*Gute Nacht.*'

'*N Abend,*' they answered in an accent which did not sound German. She wondered if they were Russian as she forced herself to walk slowly down the drive, carefully concealing the usual female roll of her hips.

An instant later she had disappeared into the growing darkness.

BOOK FOUR: *THE LAST BATTLE*

'I want you to let me take my Corps and attack across the Vistula. Damn their politics over there, Konstantin, *they're Poles!*'

General Berling, Commander 2nd Polish Corps to Marshal Konstantin Rokossovsky, Marshal of the Soviet Union, September 21st, 1944.

CHAPTER 1

General Zygmunt Berling, Commander in Chief of the Communist Polish Corps fighting with the Red Army on the Vistula, faced Marshal Rokossovsky across the big deal table. It had taken some courage to ask for this meeting, but he couldn't let the men he had once served with, fought with, caroused with, die like that, just across the river.

'Konstantin,' he began hesitantly, 'won't you let me — just with my own people — my own Corps?'

Marshal Rokossovsky stared at the bald-headed Pole with his curiously light eyes and took another puff at his long Russian cigarette before saying: 'Let you do what?'

Berling sighed. He had been serving with the Russians for three years now, ever since they had released him from the Siberian camp into which they had placed him after the 1939 surrender, and told him to form a Polish unit from the thousands of Polish prisoners in their hands. He still could not get used to their mannerisms. In the Polish Officer Corps it had always been the tradition to think and act fast; they had learned it from their French instructors after World War One. But the Russians were different; their officers always pretended stupidity and they never seemed to be able to make up their minds swiftly. Berling knew it was a defensive mechanism; they were all of them — from under lieutenant to marshal of an army — so afraid of that monster in the Kremlin that it took them an age to make up their minds, make a decision. All the same the mannerism irritated him beyond measure. Still he forced himself to be calm.

'Konstantin, we have known each other for a long time now. I have served you loyally these last years, haven't I?'

Rokossovsky nodded, but said nothing. He smoked on, watching the lazy blue smoke rings ascend to the dirty flaking ceiling, attentively.

'So, Konstantin, I deserve a favour … I want you to let me take my Corps and attack across the Vistula.' His hard face contorted suddenly, with emotion. 'Damn their politics over there, Konstantin, *they're Poles*! I can't just sit here on my fat arse with thirty thousand Poles at my command and allow my countrymen to be slaughtered like that — only a matter of kilometres away!'

The long-faced Marshal of the Red Army slowly took the cigarette from his mouth and said: 'Warsaw is not important. You know that Zygmunt?'

'I know … I know,' Berling answered desperately. 'And I agree. But I'm not talking about the city — I'm talking about people, Poles, human beings, my friends.'

'One doesn't fight battles to help one's friends,' the Marshal observed.

Berling ignored the remark. Urgently he leaned across the table and lowered his voice although the conference room at the HQ was empty. 'Listen, Konstantin, you know well what I mean. You were in the camp with me back in '40. You saw how we Poles suffered and you saw too that I didn't take the easy way out like Anders and go west. Instead I stayed behind and served Russia loyally.'

Rokossovsky nodded warily; they were treading on dangerous ground now. Even two men who were friends and had known each other for so long did not talk about the camps. 'So?'

'So. You simply can't refuse my request. Besides Konstantin, you're Polish yourself?'

Rokossovsky's pale face flushed abruptly. 'Who told you that, General?'

The Polish Corps Commander noted the change from 'Zygmunt' to 'General', but he had gone too far now. He couldn't back out any longer. 'Nobody, Konstantin. We Poles know. We know you're not like *them*,' He nodded through the window at the squat little staff officers strolling up and down in the grounds, their shoulders seemingly bowed from the weight of their heavy gold epaulettes. 'Konstantin, you are one of us. You've suffered in their camps, you've fought for them loyally in spite of what they did to you, and you know too, that in their eyes whatever you do — even if you capture Berlin single-handed — you'll still be regarded as a second-class citizen.' He pointed a trembling finger at the Marshal, almost accusingly. 'Because you are like us – *you're a Pole*!'

Rokossovsky did not respond. Suddenly he seemed to sink into himself, grow smaller, huddle together. Berling held his peace. He contented himself with watching the other man. He knew he had burnt his boats now; either he would be dismissed his Corps and perhaps even arrested, or Rokossovsky would act. Outside, two staff colonels were getting drunk in the warm late September sunshine. He watched them enviously, as they spilled a little salt on the V of skin made by their outstretched thumb and forefinger, licked it, then downed a hefty swig of the fifty procenter straight from the bottle. How he wished he could drink himself into insensibility and forget everything.

For what seemed an age, while the sun sank lower on the horizon, the Marshal did not speak. Finally, with the dusty rays of the dying sun slanting into the room almost horizontally, he said in a voice that was cold, matter of fact, almost casual. 'All right, Berling, I'll ask him.' The Pole felt a cold shiver of fear down his spine. Rokossovsky was going to ask Stalin himself!

Marshal of the Soviet Union Konstantin Rokossovsky dabbed his sweat lathered brow with a hefty dash of cologne water and took up the phone, his hand trembling violently and wet with sweat. 'Stalin here,' the voice in faraway Moscow said, low and pleasant, marred only by the strong Georgian accent, which sounded so foreign to Rokossovsky. He forced himself to forget that like most Russians he regarded the Georgians as rogues and criminals. 'Is that you Rokossovsky?'

'Yes, Comrade Stalin,' the Marshal said huskily. 'Good evening.'

'Evening, Comrade Marshal. Now then, where's the fire, eh?' At that distance, Stalin sounded like the jovial, well-wishing elderly uncle that the naïve Westerners thought him to be. But Rokossovsky, one of the hundreds of thousands of his victims, knew differently. He could visualise 'Old Leather Face' (as the Regular Army officers called him behind his back), one hand clasping his pipe, the other a glass of his favourite pepper vodka, his swarthy pock-marked face set, waiting for the moment when he could pounce on some fault, some failing and begin that terrible litany of threats, which would end with the most frightening of all; 'remember even the most important of my commanders is expendable, comrade.'

'Comrade Stalin, I thought it best to inform you,' the sweating tense Marshal began hesitantly, 'that the battle of Warsaw is nearing its end.'

'So I've heard — from *my own* sources,' Stalin replied and Rokossovsky could just hear the faint chuckle at the other end. The Georgian bastard could not refrain from letting him know that he had spies among his own staff.

'Well, Comrade, for that reason I thought it wise to call you personally and request any possible orders on the Warsaw business. I felt —'

'You acted wisely, Comrade Marshal,' Stalin interrupted him. 'You mean on account of those Polish fascists on the other side of the Vistula?' The Marshal's mouth fell open stupidly. 'Yes ... yes, Comrade, exactly.'

For a moment there was silence at the Moscow end and Rokossovsky, dabbing his streaming face with cologne, could almost hear the Soviet dictator thinking.

'Listen, Comrade Marshal, what is your estimate of their situation — the Polish fascists, I mean?'

Relieved that he had been asked a purely military question Rokossovsky answered quickly. 'Hopeless, Comrade. They're finished, they haven't a chance.'

'Excellent. So the time is ripe for our brave fellows to come to their aid, eh, Marshal?' At the Moscow end Stalin chuckled, but there was nothing humorous about the sound. To a bewildered Rokossovsky it sounded more like the throaty growl of a Russian bear about to devour its prey.

'I don't understand, Comrade.'

'Then let me explain, Comrade Marshal. After all, soldiers are not expected to be political animals, are they?'

Rokossovsky's heart missed a beat. What did the statement mean? Was it an explanation? Or was it a veiled threat? But already Stalin was going on. 'Today in their rag of a newspaper *Gazeta Warszawska*, those damned Polish fascists had the audacity to write that they 'apologised for living', blaming us for letting them down. Now, my dear Comrade Marshal, we can't let it get around that we stood by and let the *brave* —' he sneered the word '— Poles, be slaughtered by the Fritzes. The effect on world opinion would be bad. For the time being, we have to respect the opinion of those democratic idiots in the West.'

'Yes, Comrade Stalin,' Rokossovsky answered, completely bewildered by the direction of the conversation now.

'So, we shall now start to take action again, Comrade Marshal. We shall grab Warsaw, now that both the Fritzes and the Poles have conveniently fought themselves to a standstill, and at the same time we shall display the great magnanimity of the Red Army to the world, by coming to the aid of the hard-pressed Polish comrades in their hour of need.'

'You mean we go over to the offensive, Comrade?' the soldier gasped.

'I do,' Stalin answered, obviously pleased with the surprise he had sprung on the Marshal. It had not been too difficult for him to realise what Berling was doing conferring with Rokossovsky. As soon as he had received his agent's report on the Marshal's HQ that afternoon, he tumbled to what the Polish Corps Commander wanted — action. And that particular action fitted in well with his own plans for Poland. Now that there was clearly no danger that the Poles in Warsaw could set up their own government, he could afford to be generous. He would appease both the British and the Americans, and once the Polish capital had been taken he would allow his own puppet government, already waiting to move in from Russian-controlled Lublin, to take over. It would be a solution that would please everyone, except the Poles. But then, he told himself, who had ever cared about the damn Polish?

'Where, Comrade Stalin?' Rokossovsky was asking eagerly. 'Where should we put in our attack?'

'On the Vistula of course, opposite the capital. Perhaps at one of the bridges, eh? Capture one of them and establish a bridgehead on the western bank.'

'The Poniatowski, Comrade?'

'Why not,' Stalin answered casually. He knew it well from the old days in Warsaw. It would be a suitable token. The stupid masses always seemed particularly impressed when their own troops captured a bridge, he reflected.

'Comrade Stalin, may I make a request?'

'Of course,' Stalin answered easily; he knew what was coming.

'Could Berling's Polish Corps lead the attack? It would be a fitting gesture, don't you think?'

'Naturally … naturally, why not?' And then the Soviet dictator's inherent and heartless cynicism could be repressed no longer. 'After all, Comrade Marshal,' he added with a sneer, 'why not let a few more Poles die for Warsaw before we take it, eh?…'

CHAPTER 2

The great Vs of American planes caught the hard-pressed defenders of the Old City completely by surprise. One moment they were huddled behind their barricades, ready to face another day of murder and mayhem as the German field guns, firing over open sights, and the Tigers started to rattle into position at the end of every street still held by the defenders; the next the grey misery of their desperate plight was forgotten and they were staring to the west, their red-rimmed eyes hardly daring to believe what they saw coming towards them.

High, very high in the clear blue sky, trailing great white streams of vapour behind them, the 110 US Flying Fortresses advanced on the capital in perfect formation, for all the world like flights of silver birds. Below and above, the Mustangs — 146 of them — dived and twisted, jettisoning their fuel tanks which had carried them all the way from far-off England.

The German flak gunners were as surprised as the beleaguered Poles. As the defenders streamed out of their hiding places, waving their handkerchiefs and cheering wildly, the guns opened up with a crash. But it was already too late. The silver birds sailed majestically through the multi-coloured pattern of shell bursts. Suddenly thousands of red parachutes burst open like great poppies.

'Parachutists!' the throng in the streets cried excitedly. 'They're dropping the Polish Parachute Brigade!'

But they were mistaken. As the departing Fortresses flying on to the Soviet Russian field at Poltava, to land and refuel in accordance with Stalin's new policy, the Polish defenders saw that there were no men hanging at the bottom of the chutes; instead the 1,800 chutes bore urgently needed supplies.

Although many of the containers floated on the wind beyond the Polish positions and dropped into the waiting German soldiers' greedy hands, Bor was grateful. Immediately he signalled London, 'The American expedition roused enthusiasm among the population. The shelters and cellars were deserted. Everybody rejoiced that help had come and that we had not been forgotten. The spirits of the defenders have risen considerably.'

Bor had just finished dictating the message to his chief radio operator when Pelczynski burst into his Command Post, his normally grey face flushed and excited, 'General ... General,' he cried, 'can't you hear it?'

'Hear what?' Even at this late stage of the siege he was still somewhat of a stickler for military etiquette and order.

'The guns!'

'So?'

'Not the Fritzes, General,' his Chief of Staff explained hurriedly. '*The Russians!*'

'*What!*' Bor exploded.

'Yes sir,' the other man shouted joyously. 'The Russians are attacking again. They're coming to save us!'

Bor pulled himself together quickly, forcing himself not to succumb to his subordinate's heady enthusiasm. Their hopes had been raised, only to be dashed to the ground disastrously, often enough before. 'I don't know about that, Brigadier,' he said coldly. 'But we'll postpone all other operations for a further twenty-four hours and see what happens.'

'You mean the business with the Cossacks?'

'Yes,' Bor answered, raising his voice as the noise of the Red Army's softening up barrage rose to a crescendo. 'Why should the Reds help us now, when they know we're beaten?'

The enthusiasm drained from Pelczynski's face, instantly. 'I suppose you're right, sir.' He went out into the new day's battle without another word.

The two T-34s started to nose their way cautiously down the slope towards the bridge. On both sides of the pot-holed approach road, the fields were littered with the field-grey corpses of the German defenders. But the tank commanders had no eyes for the German dead; their attention was concentrated on the bridge, looming up ever larger in their periscopes. There was no sign of the enemy, but the Polish commanders were cautious men. They had been fighting the Fritzes four years now. They knew the average German was trickier than a sack full of foxes, as the Polish expression had it.

'Ditches on both sides,' the commander of the lead tank ordered. Obediently the gunner pressed the trigger of his machine gun. White tracer zipped flatly across the battle torn countryside and kicked up a dancing pattern of dirt on the ditch to their right front. Nothing! No cries of pain, no angry shouts of rage, no answering fire.

The gunner hunched his shoulder muscles and swung the smoking machine gun round to the left ditch. Again his gun rattled and a stream of slugs hissed into the dry earth. Again nothing.

The commander touched the medal of the Holy Virgin which he wore round his neck and crossed himself swiftly. Then taking a last look round in his periscope, he began to raise the hatch cover. Cautiously he popped his leather-covered head above the turret. At first he showed only the top of his head to any waiting sniper. But the half-expected slug, burning its way into his soft flesh, did not come. He displayed his pale anxious face, eyes searching the fields to both sides. But they were empty and still nothing had happened. Finally he showed his whole upper body, the broad chest, decorated with two Red Stars and the Stalingrad Medal. He stood there for one long minute — it seemed an eternity to him — as the T-34 halted, engine ticking over noisily. But if there were any of the enemy hidden on the other side of the fast-flowing Vistula they did not reveal themselves. All he could see was the flashes of scarlet fire coming from the ruins of his home town, Warsaw. In the end he decided he had risked his neck long enough. There were no enemy troops dug in at the other side of the Poniatowski Bridge; perhaps they were all occupied, destroying what was left of the Polish positions in the Old City.

Slipping behind the radio transmitter, he contacted the other tank, his rear link, who would have taken over from him in the event of his being knocked out. 'Elderberry, Elderberry... Here Strawberry ... come, come, *please*!... Over.'

Elderberry came through almost at once. Swiftly the tank commander relayed his news, ending on a completely unmilitary note, which was not catered for in R/T procedure. 'Stefan, tell the General it looks as if we're going to catch them with their knickers down. *Over and out*!'

Nearly half a kilometre away, General Alexei Bogdan lowered his binoculars from the two stationary tanks and whispered to Boris, crouching next to him in the ditch, surrounded by the waiting Cossacks. 'Well, brother, it looks as if they're going to buy it.'

Boris grinned, till it looked as if the garish pink of his face might split at any moment, and raised his pistol. 'Good, General, we'll be waiting for them. After all, the boys are getting sick of fighting civilians; they're itching to have a go at real soldiers.'

Bogdan's sole response was an abstracted grunt.

The dawn was silent save for the persistent drip-drip of raindrops from the trees. The stillness seemed unnatural — eerie — after the continuous bombardment of the last weeks. Over the silent river a low mist hung like a grey cloak. But even its wet clinging greyness could not quite conceal the soft noises that came from the other bank: the tiny jingle of pieces of equipment; nailed, booted foot scraping the side of an assault boat on the muddy shore; the soft first drip of a paddle into the dark fast-running water.

Bogdan, crouched near the rusty, dripping stanchion of the bridge, heard the noises. He took his eyes off the corpse of a woman floating swiftly down the river and nodded to Boris. Boris returned his nod and tightened his grip on the signal pistol. All around them the Cossacks, their fur caps limp with raindrops, clutched their weapons more tightly. The Reds were coming!

The two T-34s, engines roaring in low gear, started slowly to descend the incline towards the silent bridge, their drivers sweating in spite of the dawn cold, as they fought to keep the steel monsters from crashing into each other on the slippery, leaf-covered, narrow approach road. In the lead, the Polish sub-lieutenant, who had carried out the reconnaissance, swung his sloping turret round from side to side suspiciously, nerves on edge, scanning the road on both sides. But the enemy seemed to have disappeared.

His tank rattled onto the bridge, its tracks making a hell of a racket, or so it seemed to the sub-lieutenant, as it clattered over the debris left by the fleeing Germans. 'Hold tight!' the driver's voice came over the intercom, strangely distorted and unreal. He crashed through the first pathetic barrier — a pile of ration crates and an old wooden cart, and they rolled on.

They were halfway across now. 'Lieutenant,' the driver's voice broke in, 'barrier ahead!'

The sub-lieutenant gripped the turret more firmly, as the T-34 hit the pile of boxes and sent them flying in all directions. 'Good work, driv —'

The words died in his throat. Only twenty metres away, sited directly in the middle of the road, was a 57mm German antitank gun! He recognised it immediately. It was his last action. The gun roared into action and a long tongue of scarlet flame shot from its muzzle. Its trails reared high in the air with the force of the explosion.

The first shell struck the T-34 in the front boogies. It bucked crazily. The sub-lieutenant flew from the burning turret and slammed into the girders of the bridge, every bone in his body smashed. He crumpled to the wet road like a broken doll.

The Cossack gunners fired again. The solid white shell hissed terrifyingly past the stricken T-34 and hit the second one squarely in the side, as the frantic driver attempted to swing his forty-ton monster around to escape the trap. The T-34 rocked violently then with white smoke pouring from its engine, it crashed through the girders and went sailing in a wide arc into the river below and the massed assault boats of the Polish Corps.

All along the Black Cossack front the red, white and green signal flares sailed urgently into the dawn sky, as the little assault boats emerged from the grey mist. Their whole front erupted in a murderous fire. Red tracer hissed across the water at the Poles. Boats overturned, and began to sink everywhere, as the cold water poured in through the sudden holes; and abruptly the infantry were threshing the water in panic, dragged down by the weight of their equipment.

A stomach-churning howl and the Black Cossack mortar batteries joined in the slaughter. The bombs began to drop in the river, sending up huge, frightening fountains of boiling water. Still the Poles came on. The first boats hit the muddy steep bank. '*Hurrah!*' the Poles cried throatily as they attempted to scramble up, unslinging their round barrelled Russian submachine guns. They didn't get far. The Cossack fire was a solid wall of death. Bodies piled up so high on the muddy bank that the second wave had to climb over them, as if surmounting a wall, only to run into the same murderous fire.

On the opposite bank, Berling, glasses glued to his eyes, watched the slaughter in horror. Red and white tracer was sweeping the river, shooting up boat after boat, scything the infantry like a great reaper. Beyond, a handful of his men were running frantically for the nearest position, screaming and waving their weapons. But one by one, they were cut down by the cruel fire, to roll down the muddy bank and lie twitching in their death throes in the shallow blood-red water.

Now the first bullet-riddled boats were beginning to drift back filled with dead and dying. A fat corporal, his eyes wide with shock, his pudgy hand clasped over his shoulder from which blood spurted in thick jets, staggered past him, gasping, 'We didn't have a chance … not a chance!'

A Senior-Lieutenant, helmet gone, smeared with grey mud, a crazy look in his wild young eyes, attempted to report. 'With your permission, Comrade Corps Commander —' Suddenly he keeled over and fell dead at Berling's feet. The General stared at his back in horror and repulsion; the flesh was torn completely away and through a huge hole he could see the white ridged back bone.

'My God,' his Chief of Staff whispered. 'My God!'

Berling fought back his nausea. His Corps was being slaughtered on the Vistula. Abruptly with the overwhelming clarity of a vision, he knew why Stalin had granted him permission to attack. He had known the Germans would be waiting for the Corps. The attack had been nothing more than a gesture, a concession to world opinion. Red Poles trying to break through the German positions to rescue the White Poles. In spite of the latter's reactionary political creed, it would look good in the headlines of the capitalist press.

'What are we going to do, Comrade General?' his Chief of Staff asked in a low strained voice, as the last wave of assault infantry received the full weight of the enemy fire, with boats sinking everywhere and frantic men threshing the blood-red water, trying in vain to save themselves.

'*Do!*' Berling roared. '*This!*' He snatched the signal pistol from his Chief of Staff's belt, raised it and fired the first green flare high into the air.

It was the signal to withdraw. The Polish attack had failed.

One day later a stony-faced Marshal Konstantin Rokossovsky relieved General Berling of his command of the 1st Polish Corps. Stalin's publicity exercise was over. There would be no more attacks on the Vistula. The Polish fascists in Warsaw would be left to their just fate...

CHAPTER 3

On the last day of September, General Bor summoned Roswitha Jankowski to his Command Post in the cellar. She left the wounded in the crowded sewer, where she had been trying to treat them with the only resources at her disposal — paper bandages, aspirins, and vodka. Stumbling over the corpses and the madmen, howling dementedly in the stinking darkness, she hurried to his CP.

Bor was shocked by her appearance. The youthful bloom had gone from her face. There were great dark smudges under her lacklustre eyes and a tic twitched in her cheek. Still he played the gallant, as was befitting a regular cavalry officer. Bending low over her hand, he touched it with his lips, wrinkling his nose at its stench of death. 'Kiss the hand, Countess,' he said.

'General,' she answered. Just one word, as if she were too exhausted to say more.

He motioned her to a chair and beckoned the orderly with the bottle of vodka. 'A little ray of sunshine in the stomach, Countess?' he suggested.

She shook her head slowly.

He shrugged and took a glass himself, swallowing it in one gulp, then dismissed the orderly. They were alone; it was better that way. 'Countess,' he began without further preliminaries. 'Yesterday I radioed Marshal Rokossovsky — after the failure of his attack on the Vistula — that if I received no further support from him within the next twenty-four hours, I should be forced to begin talks with the Germans. You understand?'

he added after a moment when he saw that there was no answering light in her eyes. *'We are preparing to surrender!'*

Slowly, very slowly she nodded, as if it were no longer important.

Bor knew the look. He saw it all around him now. His people were exhausted, not only physically, but emotionally. They had seen too much, done too much, suffered too much. Their emotions were blunted; nothing was able to stir, to shock them any more.

'But before we start talking to the Fritzes, Countess,' he said slowly, as if talking to a small, not very intelligent child, 'we want to get those out who can still fight and want to do so.' He clenched his fist until it hurt to prevent himself being carried away by the strength of his own feelings on the subject. 'We must ensure that our youth continues the fight for Poland.'

'How?' she asked tonelessly.

'We are hemmed in — as you know — on all sides, now, Countess. There is the river of course, but I doubt if even our strongest young men could cross it in the state they are at present. To the north, and west, there is no hope for them. They would have to contend with that bandit Dirlewanger and his murderers. They would be slaughtered without mercy. The only escape route left to us is here.' He traced the route with a dirty forefinger on the big wall map of Warsaw. 'Through the sewers leading from the Old City, through the Powisle suburb into the City Centre and coming up in the Mokotow suburb — here.'

For the first time since she had entered the CP, her red-rimmed eyes showed some animation. 'But that area is held by the enemy too,' she protested weakly.

'I know. By General Bogdan's Cossacks to be exact. That is why I have asked you to come here today.'

He bent forward and started to explain his plan, while she listened, her worn beautiful face expressionless. Finally he was finished. 'Well, Countess,' he asked, 'are you prepared to undertake the mission?'

It took her a long time to make up her mind; and Bor could understand why. If she accepted it and were caught, she had signed her own death warrant. Then, as the German guns started the last barrage of the day, she nodded her head slowly. 'Yes, I'll go, General,' she whispered.

Behind her ancient guide, waving his hissing white carbide lamp from side to side, as they moved towards the river, she waded slowly through the revolting slime of the sewer, trying to keep her gaze fixed on his ragged back or the lime caked dripping walls.

They were coming ever closer to the furthest extent of the Polish perimeter now. The teenage sentries, mouths muffled in homemade cotton wadding masks, were becoming fewer, as were the dead. But in their place the rats were getting more numerous. The old man's carbide lamp threw their monstrous shadows on the walls at every new turn in the sewer and the darkness ahead was full of the eerie scampering of their feet.

'Lot more of them about nowadays,' the old man explained cheerfully in his cracked voice. 'Plenty of grub for them, of course.' He chuckled as if at some unspeakable private joke. 'Surprising the things they find to nibble down here since the siege began.' Behind him, Roswitha fought back the desire to begin screaming, just in time.

They plodded on. Time passed leadenly. To Roswitha, it seemed they had been down in that terrible sewer for ever. Once the old man stopped suddenly, whipped off his tattered jacket without explanation and flung it over her head. 'It's all right, woman,' he grunted. 'Just don't try to look.'

A few moments later she could hear a demented howling and unearthly whining like that of some dying wild animal, caught inextricably in a man-trap. The screams, magnified by the echo, were almost too much to bear. The old man understood instinctively. He pressed the jacket tighter about her head, trying to blot out the sound.

'Make way there,' she heard a voice command. 'We're coming through now.'

There came the sound of many slow-dragging feet splashing through the mire. Bodies pushed, brushed by her. An uncannily disembodied voice died away in the distance, bearing its chant of '*look, he's alive — he's smiling ... look, he's alive — he's smiling ... look...*' And then finally the procession of ghastly phantoms disappeared into the darkness and the old man released his hold on her, saying gently: 'Cracked — every one of them cracked like an old pisspot.' He tapped a gnarled finger to his temple, and resumed the journey.

Half an hour later, the waist-high, bubbling hot mess began to give way to cold water. Blessedly the stench started to disappear. 'We're getting near the river,' the old man explained. 'Not much longer now, woman.'

Five minutes passed. The sewer began to grow larger. A thin grey light filtered in from somewhere. The water flowing around her ankles was suddenly very cold. She shivered. The old man chuckled and extinguished his carbide lamp. 'Don't worry, woman,' he said softly. 'You'll soon be warm — where you're going!'

Carefully, his back pressed against the sewer's rough, dripping wall, he edged himself ever closer to the iron grating which barred their progress. 'We won't be able to get through that,' she objected, trying to keep her teeth from chattering.

'Don't you worry about that, woman,' the old man said softly. 'It ain't as solid as it looks,' He bent down and with a soft grunt, grabbed hold of the heavy grating with his arthritic hands. The grating came away with surprising ease. 'Balsa wood,' he explained with a chuckle. 'Light as a feather. Fooled the Fritzes that way a couple of times, woman.'

He lodged the fake grating carefully at the side of the sewer and beckoning her to follow, began wading into the Vistula. Minutes later, cold and trembling, she was crouching on the bank of the river, while the old man, pistol in hand, checked the path she would take to Bogdan's schoolhouse HQ.

'Nothing,' he reported in a whisper when he returned. 'The Russkis have bedded down for the night. Like their kip the Russkis do, always have. Beds, booze and brides — that's what they like. Pity there isn't enough of 'em in their own damned country, then perhaps they'd leave us poor Polacks alone.'

In spite of her coldness, Roswitha could not help smiling at the old man's easy analysis of Russian imperialism. She slipped her frozen fingers into her pocket and pulled out a silver fifty Zloty piece. 'Here, old man,' she whispered, 'for you with thanks.'

He pushed it back at her indignantly. 'I'm not doing this for money, woman,' he growled. 'I'm doing this for Poland.' Suddenly he took off his hat and bending down low, kissed her dirty frozen hand. 'Kiss the hand,' he exclaimed. 'And the best of luck.'

Moments later he had disappeared the way he had come; and she was alone in the fields that bordered the river. For a moment she hesitated, listening to the night sounds of the river and the soft plops of the water rats going about their business;

then she pressed the hard butt of the little pistol which Bor had given her personally, as if to comfort herself, before setting off into the night. In an instant the darkness had swallowed her up and she was on her way to her own personal date with destiny.

CHAPTER 4

Roswitha had planned her approach before she entered the darkened school grounds. Now with her hair combed and her shoes cleaned of the sewer's mire in a puddle of rainwater, she walked boldly up to the entrance of Bogdan's HQ.

The two young Cossack sentries recognised her as she had hoped they would. 'Is the General in his quarters?' she asked, as she had done often enough before in the last weeks.

'Yes, Citizeness,' the taller of the two Cossacks answered, using the old-fashioned form of address, recognising her as the Divisional Commander's Polish mistress. 'He has just eaten.' He grinned abruptly, half-knowing, half-bashful. 'But he is not yet in bed.'

She gave him a smile and walked by them, keeping to the middle of the steps so that they wouldn't smell the stench of the sewers on her clothes. The sentries winked at each other, as she thrust back the heavy felt blackout curtain and entered the HQ.

The hall was empty save for a few orderlies and HQ runners, their uniforms stained white with dust, smoking and chatting softly with one another. No one took any notice of her. Casually she started to climb the stairs to the ex-director's office, which was now Bogdan's bedroom. The climb seemed to take a long time and to overcome the nervousness, which made her want to run up them get it over, she concentrated her gaze on yellowing, flyblown photos of long dead schoolboys — Kickers '28 receiving sports trophy at Cracow'; a bearded stern face, looking at her, full of nineteenth-century confidence, 'Dr Stefan Bandera led the school in his God-fearing manner'; the list of 'Scholars of this School who died a hero's death for the Cause 1920/21...' The stairs seemed never-ending. At any moment she expected someone to call from below: 'Hey, you up there, where do you think you're going?'

But no call came and at last she was hurrying down the dark corridor she knew so well, her heart beating like a triphammer, not seeing — in her haste — the dark Mongol face staring at her back with a look of absolute disbelief.

The bullet pocked door of his room loomed up. For the first time since she had entered the schoolgrounds, she hesitated. Then she took a deep breath and struck it with her fist. In the heavy night silence of the school, it sounded like the knell of doom. From within Bogdan's bass voice boomed: 'Come!'

Standing there at the door, facing him in the dark red light of the room, she began her story like a fairy-tale. 'Once upon a time, General, there was a woman who cared only for her position in society and her profession. Suddenly in 1939 she realised she wasn't just an individual with responsibility for herself only — she was a member of a nation. A nation which had been treated like an orphan for centuries because it had stood in the path of great nations moving backwards and forwards over the face of Europe. That September, the woman became a patriot, who knew or cared for nothing but Poland.'

Then Bogdan, his lean face still stern and unyielding, asked her to sit down, offered her a cigarette wordlessly, and with a non-committal nod indicated she should continue with her story. She did so, eager to lay bare her soul to him at last, explaining how she had worked for the Secret Army from the day it had been formed, using her position in German military hospitals to obtain information about the Nazis by offering her body to her German superiors if necessary. She held back nothing. The words poured from her lips. She told him that as soon as Bor's Intelligence had learned the Black Cossack Division was to be used against the insurgents, she had been planted in the Hospital for the very purpose of meeting him. She shrugged. 'Well, you know what happened!'

Bogdan muttered angrily in Cossack dialect, which she did not understand, and she hesitated, wondering whether she should go on. But he waved his hand at her irritably to indicate she should continue.

She hurried on, telling him how she had been arrested by the Gestapo men; how she had been raped by their chief and how she had been forced to murder two of them in order to escape back to the Polish lines.

'Bastards — the Fritz bastards!' Bogdan exclaimed through gritted teeth. 'A clean death like that was too good for them. They should have had their eggs sawn off with a blunt sabre!'

Now it was her turn to throw up her hand to stop him. Her lethargy of the last few days had vanished now; her eyes gleamed with new energy. 'It doesn't matter, Alexei,' she said, daring to use his first name again. 'That's history. It doesn't matter. What matters now is that you help me.'

'Help you?' His stern look had vanished; but there was still a trace of caution on his face. 'How do you mean, Roswitha?'

'Alexei, General Bor is going to surrender to the Germans. He knows that he'll receive no help from the Russians now. Like the Germans, they *want* to see him defeated.'

Bogdan nodded, but said nothing.

'But Alexei, General Bor is not prepared to allow our youth to be locked away in the Fritz cages. He will surrender the old and wounded. But the young must survive. They are too precious. They are all Poland has,' she caught herself in time, before she was carried away by a wave of emotionalism. 'They must fight on.'

'And how does your General Bor propose to do that? You Poles are surrounded. There is no way out, that I know of, Roswitha.' Bogdan shrugged. 'You are trapped in that Old City of yours.'

'Yes,' she answered eagerly. 'So it would seem, but the General has a plan.' Swiftly she explained what Bor had in mind and ending, looked at him expectantly, willing him to say yes.

Slowly General Bogdan turned his head so that she should not see the conflicting emotions in his hard lean face. 'You mean I should allow your young people to escape through my lines?'

'Yes, Alexei.'

'But that would be treachery, Roswitha,' he said harshly. 'I should be betraying my German friends! Your young men would fight against us again, once they had recovered and found new positions. You know that — you *must*!'

'No,' she corrected him softly but firmly. 'They would fight not just against the Fritzes, but against all enemies of Poland. German, Russian, even Polish, if the need arose.' She saw how his big shoulders slumped slightly, as if in defeat, and she pressed home her advantage. 'Alexei,' she urged, 'it will be only a matter of perhaps five hundred young men. A night's work at the most. One little night when you will have to ensure that your men look the other way. They will emerge from the sewers at the Vistula, pass through your front, and vanish. The Germans will never know. How should they? They have no idea how many of us there are in the Old City. When General Bor surrenders, the Fritzes will assume that all the Polish defenders of the Old —'

'*Be quiet!*' Bogdan's harsh voice cut into her fervent pleading with the authority of a man who had been giving orders for nearly thirty years — and having them obeyed.

She stopped speaking, her mouth still opened, her gleaming eyes fixed on his back.

Slowly, very slowly, his big shoulders straightened as he drew himself up to his full, impressive height. He began to turn and as he did so, she knew already that she had lost.

But as that hard, unyielding, final 'No' started to form on Bogdan's lips, the door crashed open and a dark-uniformed figure, pistol in hand, almost fell into the room.

It was Obersturmbannführer Viktor Teufel!

CHAPTER 5

For one long moment they froze — the pale, blonde Polish Countess, the hard-faced Cossack General, and the black-clad SS officer, pistol clenched in his hand. There was no sound save the loud metallic ticking of the old school clock on the wall above Bogdan's bed.

Teufel's mouth was curved in a triumphant sneer, his eyes glaring, the hand which held the pistol trembling slightly — not from fear but from anger. He opened his mouth to speak, but no words came. The intensity of his anger was momentarily too great for him to speak. Finally he gasped out, 'I knew ... I knew,' straining his neck as if his collar were choking him. 'I knew ... it would end like this, you Cossack swine!'

Bogdan licked his dry lips. He had seen men like this before: men who could not stand the strain of war any longer and fled into the refuge of madness. 'What do you want, Obersturmbannführer?' he asked coldly, impassively, knowing that at the first sign of anger on his part, Teufel would press the trigger. With such men one had to remain in control.

Teufel ignored him. His burning gaze fixed on Roswitha's pale, frightened face. 'So you escaped after all, you Polack bitch, eh?' he hissed through gritted teeth. 'And now you're back at your dirty game, subverting our people. Not that you had to work hard on him' — he indicated Bogdan with a wave of his pistol — 'the two of you Slav swine were in the plot right from the start.'

Anger conquered Roswitha's fear. 'So it was you who betrayed me to the Gestapo!' she cried.

'Of course,' he sneered, lips drawn back. 'Did you think it was that weak sentimentalist von Kranz? No, he hasn't the guts for that! It was I, Viktor Teufel. But by God, I wish I had finished the job myself!' He laughed crazily. 'But it's still not too late, is it?'

'You —'

Bogdan froze her with a fierce look. 'Teufel,' he commanded firmly, his voice still devoid of emotion, 'put that pistol down! I'll take care of this business myself. The Countess came here to make a proposition to me on behalf of General Bor. I turned it down. Now I shall have her arrested.' He reached out his big hand, as if he were about to take the weapon from the Obersturmbannführer.

Teufel took a half-step backwards and jerked up the muzzle of his pistol in warning. 'Keep your big paws to yourself, Bogdan,' he screamed. 'Or you'll get it before she does.' He laughed when he saw the look in the Cossack General's eyes. 'Oh, yes, Bogdan, I'm going to shoot you as well as the Polish bitch. There are going to be no mistakes this time.'

'But the Division?' Bogdan said urgently.

'We'll find other commanders. Our camps are full of Slav stooges, who will do anything we want for a handful of silver. You are not unique, you know, *General* Bogdan.'

'The Division would not obey anyone else, Teufel,' Bogdan objected. 'You would be cutting off your nose to spite your own face, man. Kill me and you'd have ten thousand rebellious Cossacks on your hands.'

'So!' Teufel shrugged carelessly. 'What do we Germans care for the feelings of a bunch of half-wild Cossack cowboys? Dirlewanger's men would turn their machine guns on them at the drop of a hat and enjoy the slaughter. It would make a change from the Poles!' He gave his manic laugh and as the word 'Pole' reminded him of the woman, he spun round, his knuckles whitening with the pressure of his grip on the pistol's butt. Slowly the muscles of his jaw hardened. Bogdan could see them moving beneath the skin. '*Teufel*,' he cried desperately, '*No!*'

Too late! Teufel's pistol exploded shatteringly. Eyes wide with horror, Bogdan saw the sudden bloody hole appear on Roswitha's right breast. Teufel fired again, laughing as he did so. The impact of the bullet at that range spun Roswitha right round and hid her pain-contorted face from Bogdan. Her legs began to crumble slowly beneath her, as she fought death.

'Now, *you*, Cossack!' Teufel cried hysterically and pressed the trigger just as Bogdan launched himself forward. The bullet missed the General by centimetres. Exploding against the wall, it showered Bogdan's broad back with dust and plaster as his big hands sought and found Teufel's throat. The Obersturmbannführer fired again. Bogdan did not even notice the sudden pain in his side. His whole attention was concentrated on the crimson colour which suffused Teufel's face, as the SS officer squirmed furiously, trying to free himself from that killing pressure. In vain! The pistol dropped from Teufel's hand. Bogdan's ears were full of the harsh, gasping breathing of the dying man clenched in his iron grip, his eyes bulging wildly from the purple face.

Teufel tried to knee him, but Bogdan avoided the blow easily and exerted fresh pressure. Teufel was making little throaty gurgling sounds now, one hand flailing the air weakly, the veins standing out on his forehead. '*Please ... please...*' he croaked frantically, the madness in his eyes now replaced by abject fear. '*Let me go ... please!*'

But Bogdan had no mercy. He knew Roswitha must be dead. At that range, Teufel's two slugs must have ripped her body apart. He increased the pressure, sweat dripping from his forehead, his big hands digging ever deeper into the SS officer's skinny neck.

Teufel seemed to take a devil of a time to die. He hung on and on, mouth wide open, his tongue hanging out like a dog, gasping for breath.

'By the Holy Virgin of Kazan!' Bogdan cried, his chest heaving as if he were running a great race, '*croak — croak, you devil*.'

As if in answer to his demand, Teufel's spine arched and his body almost tore itself free from Bogdan's grip with the force of its death throe. Abruptly it went limp, the eyes rolled upwards to reveal the whites, and he was dead at last.

Bogdan let the dead SS officer fall to the ground, and swaying drunkenly, his face desperate, he staggered over to the woman lying crumpled in the corner.

'Roswitha,' he cried despairingly, 'speak to me.' Gently he turned her over. Her eyes stared sightlessly, a little trickle of bright red blood ran down her white cheek.

'*No!*' he moaned in an ecstasy of pain. 'No, Roswitha.'

He seized her in his big scarred arms and pressed her dead face close to his bleeding chest, rocking her from side to side with the intensity of his grief, moaning the one unbelieving word over and over again. 'No … no … no…!'

It was thus that Peter von Kranz found him, as he finally opened the door, blocked by Teufel's dead body, and stared wild-eyed at the terrible scene in front of him: the wounded Cossack General, tears streaming down his grief-contorted face, cradling the dead Countess's blonde head in arms that were red from the blood escaping from her open mouth.

Very slowly, he put his pistol back into its holster and kicked the door closed behind him to shut off the scene from the aghast eyes of the sentries.

For a moment he stood there motionlessly. Then, almost casually, he bent down and pressed his hand against Teufel's heart, averting his eyes away from the SS man's distorted face. There was no beat. Teufel was dead — and it was obvious how it had happened. Again von Kranz hesitated. Instinctively, he knew what had happened — Teufel for some reason, had shot the woman and Bogdan had killed him in revenge.

'General!'

Bogdan did not seem to hear. Kneeling there, he continued to rock back and forth on his heels, completely absorbed in his paroxysm of grief.

'General, what happened?' Peter von Kranz raised his voice. Still Bogdan did not reply.

He realised he had to act quickly, if he were to save the grief-stricken General from Himmler's revenge. Leaving Bogdan still kneeling there, he opened the door sufficiently to let four of the guards to enter, their rifles slung, now that they realised there was no danger to their beloved commander. 'Now listen, get this body down the back stairs. And as little noise as possible, understand?'

The youth who had spoken to the Countess when she'd entered the schoolhouse HQ, took his eyes off the dead woman and asked: 'And what then, Colonel?'

'Dig a grave *quick* ... behind those firs at the end of the drive and bury him. When you've done that, I want you to cover up any traces.'

'At your command, Colonel!'

Just before they left, dragging Teufel's dead body with them, Peter von Kranz clapped his hand to his pistol. 'And not a word of this to anyone, understand? Otherwise it'll go badly with you.'

They understood all right. With subdued and frightened faces, they left.

One hour later, Bogdan buried Roswitha Jankowski himself, refusing almost jealously to allow Peter von Kranz to help him. In silence, the one-armed German watched while Bogdan dug the hole himself, the only sound the scrape of his shovel against the soil and his broken-hearted sobs. Gently he lowered her into the shallow hole, mumbled something which might have been a prayer, crossed himself in the Russian fashion and began to fill it in again.

Then, and only then, did he turn, the tears dried now, to face Peter von Kranz. Completely unemotionally, he told the German what he was going to do before walking off into the heavy darkness, leaving Peter staring at his broad back in utter disbelief.

CHAPTER 6

The fields were as silent as the grave. As the dawn mist started to clear away slowly, the silence began to fill with half-forgotten sounds — the steady ticking of a watch, the faint rustle of tree branches, the soft lap-lap of the river. All had been drowned in the roar of the week-long battle.

Now the little group of staff officers around General Bogdan realised that this dawn would not commence with the usual terrible background music of war — the morning barrage. The Poles were already negotiating; this day the Germans would not fire. And while they negotiated with Bach-Zelewski, General Bor used the opportunity to slip his precious young men out of the battle zone. Now they waited at the exit to the sewer for the first of them to emerge, chain-smoking and a little nervous, listening to the dawn sounds, as if hearing them for the first time.

Next to Bogdan, sitting on a fallen log of wood, von Kranz smoked cigarette after cigarette moodily. Even now he could not believe that Bogdan was going through with this act. For a time, while the Cossack General was contacting the Poles, he had rationalized that his decision was a reaction to the terrible shock which Roswitha's murder had given him. Now he saw it differently. Bogdan was doing something irrevocable. It was not just a temporary aberration; it was a final decision, which committed him to another cause. Suddenly he maintained his silence no longer, although he had sworn to himself that he would keep his mouth shut, go through this act of treachery, get drunk afterwards to forget it, and carry on as if it had never happened. 'General,' he heard himself say suddenly.

Bogdan slowly turned his head in the German's direction. 'Yes, Peter?'

'Do you fully realise what you are doing?'

Bogdan nodded and took his time answering, as if he had to convince himself first before he could put the thoughts into words. 'Yes, Peter,' he said softly. 'I'm giving their young people a chance. It is ... the least I can do for her.' He broke off suddenly.

For a moment they listened to the harsh dawn chorus of rooks as the first pink flush appeared on the horizon. Then Peter pointed with his one hand to the Black Cossacks, dug in around the entrance to the sewer, to prevent any stray German troops from interrupting the planned escape operation. 'But General, this is,' he hesitated over the word, 'treachery. You are betraying the trust that General Bach-Zelewski put in you.'

Bogdan looked at him coldly, in silence. Suddenly von Kranz was desperate. Germany could not afford to lose the Black Cossacks. When the Red Army started to advance into Poland again, which it would surely do any day now, Germany would need every division to stop the Red steamroller crushing everything before it on its way to the frontier of the Reich. 'But General — *Alexei*,' he hissed, 'you can't go it alone. Germany needs you, but you need Germany more.' He licked his lips and blundered on. 'If Germany made you, it can ... can break you, too!'

The Cossack General looked at the one-armed German's honest face as if he were seeing it for the very first time, encouraged to say what he had to say by the German's clumsy threat.

'Peter, you are a good man, an honest man, and I owe you very much. Without your courage, your initiative in pulling me out of Kazan Concentration Camp, I might well be dead now.

I shall always be grateful to you for that. But that was in 1942, another time, when I still had hope that things could be altered, forced into the pattern I had in mind for them. This is 1944, a different year, and I know that that is impossible. There will be no return to our Quiet Don.' He said the words completely without emotion. 'Somehow or other we shall have to carve ourselves a new destiny — though God knows what it will be. But that destiny cannot include you, Peter.' His harsh voice softened a little. 'Peter, you belong to them.'

Peter von Kranz recoiled physically, as if the General had struck him across the face. The 'them' hit him very hard. It placed him squarely in the ranks of the cranks, the freaks, the racial fanatics, who had grouped themselves around Heinrich Himmler. After two years at Bogdan's side, the General was preparing to relinquish his only real contact with the good Germans. 'But ... but you can't mean that, Alexei?' he said desperately.

But Peter von Kranz was fated never to receive an answer to his question. In that same instant, two Poles, wearing World War One helmets, the red and white armband of the AK around their ragged sleeves, raised their heads cautiously above the bushes surrounding the sewer.

Boris threw his cigarette away hastily. 'Here they come, General,' he called.

The Poles stared at the waiting Cossacks nervously, their hands clutching their captured Schmeissers. But Boris told them in broken Polish that everything was all right; the operation could begin.

Moments later the long procession of Poles started to emerge from the sewer. To Bogdan and von Kranz watching them file by wearily on their way to the dense forests of the south and new hiding places, they looked like men from another world; as if the sewer were spewing them forth from hell itself. With their paper bandages caked with black blood and pus, too weary to drive off the big, greedy bluebottles swarming over them, they trudged past the silent, awed Cossacks, kept going only by their devotion to the cause of Poland.

For a while longer, they would fight the Germans. Then it would be Poland's new masters — the Russians.

Finally they would begin to fight their own people. The years would pass. They would grow older and fewer, hardly knowing why they were fighting anymore. Year after year they would be paid by American money and when the Americans grew tired of paying, by those same Germans who had raped their country so many years before. Finally they would be rounded up, one by one, wretched, ragged outcasts, half wild from their years in the forests, to be shot in the dripping cellars of some police barracks by their own people, who hated them as much as they had once hated the old occupiers.

But that was still the future. This day, as they staggered south, their eyes large and glittering in emaciated faces, they were still General Bor's heroes, escaping from German captivity to fight on for Poland's freedom. And as General Bogdan watched the long weary column straggling southwards into the grey gloom of the new day, he could not help but feel sympathy for the men who had been his enemies up to now; for they, too, like his own Black Cossacks, were fighting for their rights as a people.

'General!' Boris's voice broke into his reverie urgently. 'Look up there — on the road!'

Bogdan swung round. There was movement on the narrow, cobbled country road leading up to the sewer. He jerked up his glasses and focused them hastily. Boris and Peter von Kranz did the same.

Peter von Kranz gasped with horror. A half-track, armed with a flamethrower gun, had slid into the round calibrated glass, and on its sides it bore the double rune of the SS. Behind it was another half-track, followed by a platoon of cautious infantry. It was a German patrol!

'Dirlewanger's killers,' Bogdan snapped, one hundred per cent the General again, all indecision gone now. 'They'll run into us in five minutes if we don't do something.'

'I've got a troop armed with Molotov cocktails up in that fir wood. I thought we might have trouble from marauding Fritzes, now that the ceasefire has been sounded. I made preparations for such an eventuality. They're probably out looking for loot, knowing them,' Boris explained quickly.

Von Kranz stared at the two men, whom he had known so long, incredulously. 'But General,' he cried desperately. 'They might be Dirlewanger's thugs, but they're Germans too! Can't you understand that? They're Germans — *my fellow countrymen!*'

Bogdan was not listening. Swiftly he snapped an order at Boris, who reacted at once. He slung his binoculars around his neck and crouching low began to double swiftly towards the Cossacks hidden in the woods.

'General!' von Kranz cried. '*Stop him*! For God's sake! I can't stand here and watch my own people walk into a trap.' His voice broke, 'I can't do that, even for you, Alexei!'

Bogdan stared ahead, his face stony; seeming not to hear Peter von Kranz's desperate, frantic plea. Peter flung a tortured glance at the road. Dirlewanger's men were walking carelessly into the trap. They were not even taking elementary precautions now; their postures were completely relaxed. They had swung round the corner without trouble. Now they obviously felt that the first houses of the Mokotow suburb were empty — were theirs for looting. In the half-tracks, the masked flamethrower operators were beginning to light cigarettes, contrary to all regulations. If the Cossacks caught them now, it would be a massacre.

Peter put his one hand on Bogdan's arm. He flung it off angrily and the German knew that the two-year friendship between them, started that winter in Kazan Concentration Camp, was over. The Cossack General had decided to go his own way at last. The words he was about to speak died on his lips.

Abruptly he made his decision. He broke away from the little group of staff officers and crouched low, started to pelt towards the unsuspecting Dirlewanger's. Bogdan's
hand fell to his pistol. Swiftly he aimed, the muzzle pointed directly at the German's broad back. His finger curled round the trigger. '*Stop* … *STOP, YOU DAMNED FOOL!*' he bellowed angrily.

Peter von Kranz continued running across the open fields, screaming his warning to the advancing Dirlewanger's. Bogdan pressed the trigger and then with a muttered curse, he lowered the Luger. His staff officers stared at him in pale-faced, shocked expectancy, waiting for him to give them the order to fire.

Up ahead the Dirlewanger's had come to a sudden halt, startled by the sudden appearance of a German officer from nowhere. They began to unsling their weapons, crouching instinctively, knowing that the one-armed officer's unintelligible, yet urgent words signified trouble.

The hidden Cossacks waited no longer. Just as von Kranz sprang onto the road, waving his hand at the Dirlewanger's, frantically urging them to move back, the first Molotov cocktail sailed through the morning air. It exploded just in front of the running man. For a moment nothing happened as the petrol splashed up at his clothes. Then the charge went off. There was a muffled crump. A sheet of red flame, tinged with black oily fumes shot up. At once von Kranz's uniform began to burn fiercely. The German tried to beat the flames out with his single arm. He writhed and jerked convulsively, trying to escape their stifling, searing horror. But there was no escape.

As the Cossack machine guns opened up with a high-pitched, hysterical hiss and firebombs exploded on the sides of the two half-tracks, Peter von Kranz, blinded by the ever-mounting flames, staggered forward a few paces, his outstretched arm burning furiously.

Bogdan choked back his cry of anguish as the German stumbled, fell to his knees, tried to rise, then slumped to the road, his body almost consumed by flames now. 'Come on — *we must save him!*' he roared, attempting to dart forward, but two of his staff officers caught him just in time.

'No, General,' they yelled above the screams of the burning Dirlewangers. 'No … it's no good. Can't you see — you can't save the Fritz officer now!'

Bogdan knew they were right. Peter von Kranz lay perfectly still on the road, while fifty metres away his fellow countrymen were being slaughtered by the triumphant young Cossacks, his rapidly blackening horror of a head in a puddle of flickering blue flame. A moment later the napalm tank of the first half-track exploded. A vicious jet of scarlet flame hissed down the road and enveloped it in furiously burning fire.

When it finally disappeared, there was no trace of Peter von Kranz left, save a heap of random bones, gleaming white against the black of the bubbling tarmac. The German, who had created the Black Cossacks, had disappeared so completely that he might well never have existed.

Alexei Bogdan was freed of his final German contact at last...

BOOK FIVE: *THE RECKONING*

'There is no way back. We must march west. The Nazi Empire is breaking up. It is only a matter of months now; then there will be land for the taking for those who are brave and bold.'

General Alexei Bogdan to Major Boris, 3rd October, 1944.

At eight thirty precisely on the morning of October 3rd, 1944, the battle for Warsaw came to an end. General Bor and his Secret Army had fought for sixty-three days; now they could fight no more.

That morning a heavy curtain of silence suddenly descended upon the shattered, burning Old City. All that could be heard was the steady crackle of flames and the abrupt, rending crash, as yet another wall or roof crashed to the ground.

As far as the eye could see, there was nothing but death and destruction. Now the Polish capital presented a picture of sordid horror. The streets were blocked with great piles of brick and rubble. Lamp standards, twisted into impossible shapes, were silhouetted stark black against the burning sky. A great stench hung over the city, composed of the sickly sweet smell of gas from the ruptured mains and the stench of dead, lying everywhere like abandoned bundles of rags.

Rags tied over their mouths against the stink, the Germans waited for the Poles to emerge from their hiding places; and at strategic spots, the survivors of the tank squadrons who had fought the long costly battle against the Poles tensed behind their guns, ready to open fire at any moment, still not believing that the insurgents were actually giving up.

At nine o'clock, the heavy tense silence was broken by the sound of many feet marching, not with the sharp military precision of confident, eager, well-fed young men; but with the worn yet dogged persistence of exhausted men who were at the end of their tether; were kept going by a sheer effort of will.

'*They're coming*!' the words flew from mouth to mouth among the waiting German infantry, hidden at every street corner, '*The*

Poles are coming!' Not even the most hard-boiled veteran among them used the word 'Polack'; the Poles had fought too long and too well for them to apply that derogatory epithet to them any longer.

The slow tramp of feet grew ever louder. Then four abreast, old and young, men and women, the lead battalion swung round the corner, the Polish eagle in their caps or the red and white armband of the AK on their sleeves. Somehow or other they had washed and shaved and cleaned up their sewer-mired uniforms; now sick and wounded, parched with thirst and half starving, they kept their slow step, heads held high, eyes staring fixedly ahead, as if they were not aware of thousands of enemy eyes gazing at them in open-mouthed amazement. Here and there a German infantryman, hardly aware of what he was doing, clicked his heels together and saluted the men, who only hours before, he had been trying to kill. Somewhere, someone sobbed.

Stolidly they marched on, the first of nine thousand Poles who would surrender that day. Past the Technical University, down burning street after street, towards the Kerceli Square, the only sound the slow, persistent stamp of their boots, as they came ever closer to the place where it would all end. They had offered their blood without stint, and they had paid dearly, victims of a heartless clash of ideologies. Behind them in the burning rubble lay the flower of Poland's youth, who had died in vain. Now they were marching out of Warsaw, which had been the tomb of their heady hopes for a free Poland, into an uncertain future. For many of them this — the burning, shattered streets of the Old City — would be the last sight of home. For on that day, though they did not realise it at the time, they were going into exile: to end their days in the foggy, smoke-enshrouded industrial cities of Northern England or the bustling concrete jungles of the American Mid-West. They would become the proud, strange old men and women, who subscribed to obscure newspapers, ate funny foods, and spoke a guttural harsh language that no one could understand.

General Bach-Zelewski and those commanders who had borne the brunt of the fighting, Dirlewanger, Bogdan and the rest, were waiting for them in the Kerceli Square. Nervously the big East Prussian fingered his newly awarded Knight's Cross, and kept staring at the entrance to the ruined square, as if even now he couldn't quite believe the Poles were actually surrendering. Dirlewanger was nervous too. But for other reasons. As soon as the Poles had dumped their weapons and had been safely marched away, he could begin the work of razing the city, as Himmler had commanded; undoubtedly there was still plenty of loot in the Old City, ruined or not. A couple of old masters, easily transportable, might buy him a ticket to Switzerland and a new passport for South America for the day when the crash came, as it would soon, and he would have to go 'underground'.

Bogdan was not nervous. He was completely still; his harsh lean face was composed and emotionless, revealing nothing of his inner turmoil. He watched a scrap of charred paper, wafted from one of the burning houses, fall slowly onto the obscene travesty of skin, bones and rags, which had once been a Polish soldier. For a moment he wished he might have been that man. But without him, his Cossacks were lost. They needed him, and he must not give way to his emotions. He must plan, act; try to save them from the fate suffered by the Poles, rescue them from the holocaust to come.

With a great cry of 'Long Live Our Polish Republic!', the Poles swung into the square and began to sing the national anthem '*Not Yet Is Poland Lost*' as they marched towards the waiting Germans, their weakened voices ringing out bravely and filling the shattered square. Dirlewanger cursed angrily and slapped his soft, beringed hand against his pistol holster. But no one paid any attention to the SS Colonel; the eyes of the waiting officers were fixed on the shabby, exhausted men and women who had defied the whole might of the Greater German Wehrmacht for seven long, terrible weeks. As the Major in charge of the lead battalion barked a command and they came to a grateful halt, Bach-Zelewski turned to his Chief of Staff and whispered incredulously, 'Heaven, arse and twine, Grez, is that what they fought with? That pathetic collection of broken-down humanity!'

Grez nodded numbly.

An instant later General Bor, accompanied by Pelczynski, drove up in a German car. '*Meine Herren*,' Bach-Zelewski barked, '*die Herren Polen*!' He stiffened to the salute, as did all the other officers, as Bor stepped out of the car, with the exception of Dirlewanger, who thrust his hands in his breeches' pockets as a sign of his contempt.

Bor, dressed in a long ankle-length civilian coat, with the red and white armband of the AK around his right sleeve, took off his felt trilby in answer.

Bach-Zelewski smiled uncertainly and offered his hand. Bor took it and bent his head in the Polish fashion. 'General,' the East Prussian began, 'let me congratulate you on your stubborn, heroic defence of the city. But your efforts were misplaced. It would have been better if you had fought side by side with us against the common enemy — the Soviet Union.'

'General,' Bor said stiffly in his Austrian German, keeping his gaze fixed on the ground, 'I would prefer not to discuss the matter, please.'

Bach-Zelewski shrugged. 'As you wish, General. Then let us begin.'

'Yes, let us get it over with,' Bor answered thickly, turning away suddenly so that the big German would not be able to see the tears in his bloodshot eyes. This moment was the bitterest of his whole long, violent life.

One by one the Poles began to advance towards the centre of the abruptly silent square. Under the wordless direction of the heavily armed Field Gendarmes, they started to toss their weapons onto the spot designated.

Abruptly the pride went out of them, as soon as they had parted with their weapons. Bogdan, watching them stony-faced, could see it drain away visibly, as if for the first time, they were realising the full implication of their actions. Shoulders bent in defeat, faces set in infinite, almost unbearable despair, they began to shuffle off down the dusty road which led to the railway station, from where they would be transported to the German prison camps.

Suddenly Bogdan could not stand the look of utter defeat on the Poles' faces any longer. He nudged his Chief of Staff. 'Boris,' he whispered, 'let's get the hell out of here! I've had enough.'

'Understood, General,' Boris replied with unusual formality, as if the scene deserved such seriousness.

In silence, broken only by the sound of the Poles shuffling west, they walked over to their waiting horses. The wizened-face, bandy-legged groom was sobbing, as if his heart were broken, the tears streaming down his cheeks.

'What is the matter with you?' Boris demanded.

The groom relinquished his hold on *Don* and pointed a trembling finger at the Poles. 'The Poles,' he sobbed, 'they're just like us Cossacks. Betrayed, they've been.' He choked. '*Betrayed!*'

'Shut up, you old fool,' Bogdan commanded. His face set and grave, revealing nothing, he swung himself onto *Don's* broad back, broken by the livid scars of the recent battle. 'We're not like them — we still have our freedom!'

Cruelly he dug his spurs into the big stallion's flanks, as if he could not get away from Kerceli Square soon enough.

Already Dirlewanger's killers were moving in to complete the work of destruction. The terms of surrender had only included members of the Secret Army, not civilians. Wherever the Dirlewangers spotted them, men, women or children, they were shot in cold-blood. Everywhere neatly stacked bodies waited for collection. Soon the centre of the Polish capital resembled one vast cemetery, inhabited solely by lean-ribbed, starving half-wild cats and dogs, tearing boldly at the corpses for food.

Dirlewanger's engineers followed. While he and his bodyguard looted, searching the ruins of the shattered great houses for what they could find, his destruction squads proceeded with the systematic demolition of the city. The first squad drilled a hole in the wall of the building to be blown up and moved on to the next one. The second squad, following them, packed the holes full of long sausages of explosives. After them came the last squad, who lit the fuses and set off the TNT. Street after street was blown up in this manner.

Advancing rapidly, Dirlewanger's crazily cackling barbarians destroyed everything in their path like a stream of human locusts. Houses, churches, museums, schools — they all went up in the air. Trees were felled; underground water mains and the sewage system were blown apart; telegraph poles struck down, tramway rails ripped up; parks seared into unrecognisable charred messes by flamethrowers. Warsaw disappeared before them.

Now nothing but death and destruction stretched to the horizon. Shattered trucks, burnt-out and contorted tanks, tangled heaps of wreckage which had once been cannon — they covered the ruined landscape like metal droppings. And everywhere lay the dead — a quarter of a million of them, a ghastly, infinite tableau of horror. Here a body without a head, or its limbs torn off. There a pile of them with the stomachs ripped open, their viscera swelling out like some terrible sea anemones. A dead claw of a hand reaching forth from a hollow as if in supplication. A pair of eyes staring up in accusation, which would continue to stare sightlessly until they rotted away in the skull. The details were repeated endlessly. Warsaw had become a great rubbish heap of ruins, rusting metal and rotting human flesh. A terrifying monument to twentieth-century technology.

But even above the last of the Dirlewanger engineers' explosions, as they completed their deadly work in Warsaw, a new roar could be heard from the East. General Bogdan standing next to Boris on the height above the Poniatowski Bridge, watched the fresh-faced seventeen-year-olds of a new German People's Grenadier Division taking over the positions of the Black Cossacks, before they were moved into Himmler's reserve. He took his eyes from the German cannon-fodder and stared at the horizon. Signal rockets were flying into the air all along Rokossovsky's front in multi-coloured prodigality, while the softening-up artillery barrage grew ever louder.

'You'd think Konstantin was celebrating,' Boris, who had once served on the Marshal's staff, remarked thoughtfully. 'As if he had achieved a victory?'

Bogdan nodded. 'But then he has, hasn't he? The Reds will start advancing again now. What have they to fear? The Poles are beaten and the Fritzes fought to a standstill. Warsaw is theirs for the taking!' He paused for a moment and watched as the green, serious-faced Grenadiers settled into the holes and dugouts vacated by the grinning, contemptuous veterans of the Black Cossacks. The Fritzes wouldn't last twenty-four hours once the Reds hit them, he told himself. 'There'll be no stopping the Red Army now, Boris. Soon they'll have Warsaw and Central Poland. After that Romania and Hungary. Eastern Poland, East Prussia will follow. Then Silesia. By Christmas they will be on the borders.' He broke off and gestured helplessly to the west.

Boris knew what his tall General meant. They would be at the frontier of the German Reich. 'And the Black Cossack Division, General? Do we march east?' he asked, forcing the issue of their future at last, blurting out the question he had wanted to ask ever since their German advisers had 'disappeared during the course of the battle', as he had reported von Kranz's and Teufel's deaths to Army HQ.

Bogdan shook his head firmly. 'No, Boris. There is no way back for us. We must march west. You see the Nazi Empire is breaking up. It is only a matter of months now and there will be land for the taking, for those who are brave and bold.' He tapped the worn hilt of his sabre. 'For those who are prepared to wield their swords and believe in their cause. Once, you know, this country of Poland was inspired from nothing by a long-haired pianist, who could hardly speak the language correctly, and a broken-down, elderly cavalryman who couldn't hold his water for more than an hour at a time. But they were bold, knew what they wanted and came along just at the right time when the Russian, German and Austrian Empires were breaking up. Soon, Boris, the same thing will happen here once again. So if we can no longer establish our Cossackia on the Quiet Don, we must carve ourselves out a new Cossackia in the west.' He fingered the little leather bag of his native soil around his neck for an instant. 'Fortune favours the bold, Boris.'

'And the Fritzes?' his Chief of Staff asked, as the Black Cossacks began to form up along the Jerozlimskie, squadron after squadron of them as far as the eye could see, ready to march off, their horses' heads tossing impatiently, as the roar of the Soviet artillery grew ever louder.

Bogdan swung himself onto the back of his horse easily. 'What do I care about the Fritzes now, Boris!' he answered. 'I'm finished with them. All that matters now is those men,' he pointed his hand at the long column of soldiers behind him. Raising himself high in the saddle, he bellowed, 'Black Cossack Division at an easy trot — *forward!*'

Their bits jingling boldly, the Black Cossack Division advanced down the broad, ruin lined avenue, eight abreast, the riders rising and falling rhythmically on their mounts, twin streams of grey breath shooting out of the horses' flared nostrils in the sudden cold, a forerunner of the bitter, harsh winter soon to come.

But General Alexei Bogdan was no longer afraid of that unknown future. At last he was free of the Germans. He was leaving the Warsaw hellhole, and behind him rode his brave Cossacks, every one of them devoted to him to the death.

A gang of drunken, shouting Dirlewangers staggered into the road and tried to bar their way, grinning stupidly, as the cavalry came closer. Bogdan looked down at them coldly and cried: '*Make way, Germans! The Cossacks are coming!*'

Even in their drunken state, the Dirlewangers recognised the light of death in the Cossack General's eyes. They fell back hastily.

Troop after troop rode by them and each new captain cried down at them contemptuously, '*Make way, Germans… The Cossacks are coming!*'

And then they were gone, out of the dead city, the thunder of their hooves dying away behind them, heading steadily westwards, determined to carve themselves out a new life in the uncertain months to come, responsible to no one or nothing, but themselves and their own heady new dreams.

THE COSSACKS WERE COMING…

A NOTE TO THE READER

Dear Reader,

If you have enjoyed this novel enough to leave a review on **Amazon** and **Goodreads**, then we would be truly grateful.

Sapere Books

Sapere Books is an exciting new publisher of brilliant fiction and popular history.

To find out more about our latest releases and our monthly bargain books visit our website:
saperebooks.com

www.ingramcontent.com/pod-product-compliance
Lightning Source LLC
Chambersburg PA
CBHW060440180626
46817CB00007B/2906